Jimbo Scott's entir... ...ble, brownish lesio... ...flogged to death, each lesion a ... ... face gaunt and wasted, as if the disease had eaten away the body from within. Dr. Robby Keough and Dr. Hampton, both dressed in racal biosafety suits, stood over the cadaver.

Hampton licked his lips. Sweat dripped from his forehead, fogging his visor. He took a scalpel from the tray at his side. His hand was trembling and he fought to control it.

"Okay," said Robby. She saw that Hampton would be of little use in this procedure. "Give me the scalpel."

She made her incision, cutting from the chest to the pubic bone. Sluggish brown blood welled up and trickled onto the stainless steel table. Robby then cracked the chest, cutting through the tough muscle surrounding the rib cage and through the lattice of bone.

Hampton gazed into the thoracic cavity as if looking into a pit of horror. "Heaven help us all," he whispered.

This was America's first sight of what was in store for it. . . .

OUTBREAK

OUTBREAK

A Novel by Robert Tine

Based on the motion picture written
by Laurence Dworet & Robert Roy Pool

A SIGNET BOOK

SIGNET
Published by the Penguin Group
Penguin Books USA Inc., 375 Hudson Street,
New York, New York 10014, U.S.A.
Penguin Books Ltd, 27 Wrights Lane,
London W8 5TZ, England
Penguin Books Australia Ltd, Ringwood,
Victoria, Australia
Penguin Books Canada Ltd, 10 Alcorn Avenue,
Toronto, Ontario, Canada M4V 3B2
Penguin Books (N.Z.) Ltd, 182–190 Wairau Road,
Auckland 10, New Zealand

Penguin Books Ltd, Registered Offices:
Harmondsworth, Middlesex, England

First published by Signet, an imprint of Dutton Signet,
a division of Penguin Books USA Inc.

First Printing, March, 1995
10 9 8 7 6 5 4 3 2 1

The single biggest threat to man's continued dominance on the planet is the virus.

—Dr. Joshua Lederberg
Nobel Laureate

PROLOGUE

Motaba River Valley

CONGO-KINSHASA, 1967

They had nothing in common but the terror they shared. There were five of them, five soldiers huddled together in a shallow slit trench, miserable and afraid, listening to the high-pitched whine of mortar shells crashing through the dense vegetation and exploding, showering them with damp muddy earth. Two of the men were black, two were white, the fifth Asian—all of them were mercenaries, soldiers of fortune culled from armies and slums, men desperate enough to risk their lives for money.

Ask them what side they were on, who or what they were fighting for, and they would not have had an answer. All they knew was that they were combatants in one of the interminable wars that sometimes raged, sometimes guttered, in postcolonial Africa.

Proxy wars, they were called, each side backed surreptitiously by one of the great powers, East versus West, wars of ideology that accomplished nothing but the establishment of a long-lived state of misery and woe.

But at that moment, political doctrine and global hegemony were much less pressing than survival. The slit trench marked the perimeter of a makeshift mercenary camp, a few acres of torn tents and tattered sandbag gun emplacements situated on the low banks of the Motaba River. The five men had been on guard duty when a sixth soldier drew enemy fire when he ventured down to the river to draw some muddy water for use in the camp infirmary.

Of course, "infirmary" was the wrong word

for the structure, implying as it did a degree of order and cleanliness. The medical facilities were even more wretched than the rest of the camp. It was nothing more than an open-sided shanty, a canvas roof covering a floor of worn and splintered duckboards, every square inch crammed with cots.

The lone doctor, a regular army medic called Raswani, and his handful of assistants stretched their meager medical supplies to the limit, trying to tend the sick and wounded. Fighting had been relatively light in recent weeks and casualties from the war had been few—yet every bed in the infirmary was occupied, disease cases, men afflicted with some mysterious malady Dr. Raswani was powerless to control.

He wrung out a wet towel and placed it on the hot forehead of a Belgian mercenary. Forty-eight hours earlier, he had been a strapping, swaggering soldier, a brute of a man, strong and heavy-limbed. Now he was scarcely more than a living corpse, his body racked by fever and eaten away by disease, every muscle, every joint was aflame with pain. His eyes were a vivid red and wild with torment. Hot sweat streamed down his face as if he had been caught in a sudden cloudburst.

The Belgian stirred feebly. *"J'aimal . . ."* He mumbled. *"Donnez moi quelque chose . . . De la morphine vous devez avoir quelque chose. De la morphine . . ."*

Raswani was, by nature, a compassionate man, but he did not have enough pain killers on hand to administer a dose to this man. It would be a waste. The Belgian would be dead soon.

"Aidez moi . . ." The Belgian tried to rise from his sweat-sodden bed, but he fell back, that small exertion depleting his tiny reserves of strength. Raswani put a thermometer between the patient's chattering teeth and checked his watch.

Raswani had spent his entire life in Africa and he knew all about the terrible tropical diseases that lurked in the lush vegetation. Dengue fever, malaria, bilharzia, yaws—poxes, fevers and viruses by the score—and he could treat almost all of them. Given the right facilities and enough drugs he could take on most of the illnesses that Africa threw at mankind and triumph. But this one was different. Raswani could feel its power and it terrified him.

He took the thermometer from the Belgian and squinted at it, the tiny gradation on the glass shaft swimming before his bleary eyes. Raswani could not remember the last time he had slept.

"Still over a hundred and six," he murmured to himself. "Why can't we bring it down?"

There was a lull in the mortar barrage, a respite from the shelling just long enough for Raswani to hear a sound he had been hoping to hear for weeks: the harsh drone of a helicopter, the machine streaking in low, flying at treetop height. As Raswani hurried to meet the chopper he allowed himself a tiny burst of hope—maybe they were being resupplied or, even better, being evacuated.

His hope turned to despair the instant he saw the helicopter as it touched down on the landing pad, kicking up a cloud of gritty red dust. It wasn't one of the big Westland HC-Mk4 that ferried supplies and troops, but a smaller Bell 47. The instant the skids hit the ground, the door opened and two figures climbed out, each dressed in khaki-colored contamination suits, their faces hidden by thick green Plexiglas shields. The suits bore no rank or national identification, but Raswani could tell that one was the superior, the other an aide. The aide carried a black doctor's bag.

"Have you brought any medicines?" Raswani asked.

"Soon," replied the leader. His voice was muffled, but his accent was American.

"Please," Raswani implored. "You have to send help." He led the visitors toward the hospital tent. "Thirty deaths yesterday, eighteen the day before. We are being wiped out. This disease is killing our men faster than enemy bullets. We need supplies: plasma, penicillin, morphine."

The three of them walked past cot after cot, a sick soldier sprawled on each. The leader stopped and looked down at one, an American mercenary. He was shivering uncontrollably, shaking in the grip of the virulent fever and looked to the leader as if he were his savior.

"Take me home, mister . . ." the soldier

gasped. "Get me outta this shithole. Please, I wanna see my girl." He tried to snatch at the leg of the suit, the leader shrinking away from his touch.

"We'll get you home, soldier," said the leader. "But first let's take a blood sample." He nodded to his aide, who pulled a syringe from his bag.

The aide swabbed down a patch of skin on the soldier's thigh and then plunged the long needle deep into his flesh, filling the cylinder with blood. He placed the syringe in an aluminum tube and sealed it.

"I'm gonna die, right?" the soldier said, his voice filled with desperation and despair. "Tell my girl I love her. Her name is Susan Teller . . ."

The leader nodded. "You'll tell her yourself, son, I promise." The lie came easily to him and it cost him nothing. The soldier would die on that bed, his body would never be found.

"I've seen enough," he said to Raswani.

"There's one more thing . . ." Raswani led the two men out of the hospital. "I think you should see this."

Behind the infirmary stood a long row of

corpses, dozens of them, stacked like cord-wood. The bodies were covered with sheets, but the dirty cloth was stained and spotted with blood.

"The men inside are in the early stages of the disease," said Raswani. "By tomorrow night he will look like this." The doctor lifted the sheet. The two visitors flinched at the sight.

"Mother of God," the aide whispered.

"Men wounded in battle we can deal with," said Raswani urgently. "But this disease . . . We need more doctors too and nurses. Suits like yours to protect us. This disease spreads too fast."

The leader nodded and then started back toward his helicopter. The pilot hadn't shut down the engines. "The planes will bring everything. Tonight."

Dr. Raswani heard the planes just after dusk. "They're coming," he said to himself. "Thank God!"

The soldiers in the camp had heard the approaching aircraft as well, so by the time

Raswani made it out of the hospital tent the makeshift runway was surrounded by jubilant servicemen. After weeks in the bush, weeks of privation and hardship, the planes suggested salvation, that they had not been abandoned to die in that terrible place.

Coming in from the west, out of the red rays of the setting sun was a lone C-47—but no one seemed to notice that the aircraft was coming in too high and too fast for a landing.

There was still enough light for Raswani and the soldiers to see the bomb bay doors open in the belly of the plane, then an object tumbling into the air. A moment later a parachute unfurled and what appeared to be a large supply crate started to float toward the earth. The soldiers were clapping and shouting, running for the spot where they expected the supplies to come to earth.

It was then that Raswani realized that it was not the relief they had been expecting—it was a bomb. He opened his mouth to scream as the explosives detonated, a huge fireball that seemed to set fire to the air itself. Ammunition and fuel dumps erupted, adding their own flames to the fire. Debris—pieces of tent, sandbags, and pieces of flesh and bone were hurled high into the air, the jungle itself was on fire, the howls of burning animals and birds mixing with the screams of dying men.

Every soldier died, their bodies charred to black ash, never to be discovered, never mourned—it was just another unremarkable massacre in a small, dirty war. But there was one survivor. Her survival skills honed by a thousand generations of jungle living, a small black-and-white colobus monkey outraced the cloud of poisonous gas and the avalanche of fire, the terrified animal retreated further into the jungle, beyond the reach of man and his relentless weapons.

1

The United States Army Medical Research Institute of Infectious Diseases, known by the acronym USAMRIID, was housed in a vast, ultra secure facility in suburban Maryland. The center was a series of low, massive, windowless structures, buildings that seemed to strive to be unobtrusive—but there was something fearsome about them, as if giving a hint of the horrors contained within.

The compound was extremely secure. The

well-tended lawns and gardens were encircled by a high steel-and-concrete fence, a barrier that was crash-proof and bomb-resistant and the gates were manned by heavily armed military policemen. It seemed that the soldiers chosen for this guard detail were selected for their single-minded devotion to duty and for their complete lack of a sense of humor. If General Billy Ford himself, commander of USAMRIID, showed up at the front gate without the proper passes, he would be sent politely, but firmly, on his way.

Security was just as tight within the buildings, with guards posted at checkpoints in the corridors. Bronze doors six inches thick separated the bulk of the facility from the labs where the hazardous materials were handled and access to these areas was severely restricted.

There were four levels of laboratories in the complex, each dealing with a different set of viruses. In the lab designated Biosafety Level One, the diseases under study were not lethal or else were not very contagious, and protective gear for the workers there was kept to a minimum.

BL-2 was much more serious. Here workers were engaged in research on salmonella, shigella, a whole cocktail of Lyme diseases and HIV-one. At this level negative air pressure was constant and protective gear—gloves, biosafety hoods—had to be worn.

HIV-two, typhus, and rocky mountain spotted fever were the diseases under investigation on Biosafety Level 3, with workers there wearing the sort of outfits one would see in an operating room, as well as complete facial protection.

Access to BL-4 was restricted to the bare smallest number of personnel on the base, the bare minimum of researchers, and doctors needed to run the lab. It was at level four that the most infectious and lethal diseases known to medicine were studied, viruses like the African strains of Ebola and Lassa and a newly discovered killer called Korean hemorrhagic fever. There were no cures or vaccines for these diseases, so on this level there was a mania for security and precaution.

Before entering the lab, proper workers had to go through an elaborate series of safety procedures. First they put on green surgical scrubs followed by three pairs of latex gloves closed and taped securely at the wrists. Over this went an all-enveloping blue space suit, a bulky, ungainly garment with a tall helmet fitted with a Plexiglas face mask. Plugged into the side of the suit was a tightly coiled air pipe that hooked into the ventilation system, the hoses running on tracks set in the ceiling.

The team that worked here were the elite of USAMRIID, a small band of professionals who dealt with deadly killers on a daily basis. The leader of the team was Colonel Sam Daniels, a short, intense, irascible man, consumed with his work—to Daniels, this was more than a job, it was a mission.

He had trained his three subordinates, two men and a woman, all three of them commissioned majors in the U.S. Army, molding them into a perfect working team. Each one of them knew their function and they performed with the efficiency Daniels expected of them. Casey Schuler was Daniels' right-hand man, working in concert with his chief like a shadow. Tom Jaffe did all the tissue sample and blood work; Roberta Keough did the pure research.

But there was a certain tension in the air that morning—the team was breaking up. Roberta Keough was departing for good. She was resigning her commission, leaving the Army, and joining the Center for Disease Control in Atlanta—the arch rival of USAMRIID.

That was bad enough, but her parting was occasioned by a divorce—her divorce from Sam Daniels. They had worked together uneasily during her last month, but Roberta, Jaffe, and Schuler would be glad when the enforced togetherness would come to an end. Sam Daniels alone could not imagine that his marriage and his team were at an end.

Daniels lived amid the disorder and clutter that had become the hallmark of the newly— and unhappily—divorced American male. Since splitting with his wife, Daniels had taken possession of a town house in Frederick, Maryland, but it couldn't be said that he had actually moved in. Other than unpacking his computer, his couch, and throwing a mattress on the floor, he had done nothing to make the house a home. The walls were bare except for a calendar and a dart board, the remainder of the pictures and photographs he had salvaged from his marriage leaned against the walls as if marking their future positions.

Piles of storage cartons were scattered here and there, some half empty and rifled, others untouched and sealed with masking tape, standing in for more substantial pieces of furniture. There were stacks of books everywhere, the constant reminder of the acrimony that had erupted during the division of the library. Neither he nor his wife could remember who had bought which volume and as they were both doctors, the books were a professional resource. The fights had been fierce, almost nastier than the breakup itself.

And yet, Daniels' reluctance to unpack was due to more than just laziness or lack of time. Somewhere in the back of his mind, Daniels knew that this Spartan set of rooms would never be home. Home was wherever his wife was; he prayed that someday he'd be going back there.

Although, even Daniels had to admit that it looked unlikely, just then anyway. Robby's mind was made up—the marriage was over—and the move to Atlanta underscored that. Not the end of the earth, but far enough to preclude his wooing her back.

For the time being, Daniels had to occupy himself with a quiet, rather monastic existence that revolved around his two huge wolfhounds, Louis and Helen, endless doses of Irish music—primarily The Chieftains, but with occasional rations of Runrig, Battlefield Band, and The Pogues—and work.

Work consumed him, it always had. It had devoured his marriage, but now it was just about all he had left. The tracking and killing diseases all over the world was an endless task. He sometimes spent weeks on the road, traveling to the remote corners of the Earth, stalking killer strains of diseases, capturing them and returning to the USAMRIID lab like a triumphant hunter. When he wasn't ranging through the disease-ridden backwaters of the world, he was in the lab. When exhaustion or hunger drove him home, he ate and slept just enough to put him back on his feet again.

Weekends were spent in front of the screen of his laptop computer, with breaks to walk the dogs and meals poured out of a can and heated in a microwave oven. But he was on call and a call on the weekend was usually bad news, particularly when Daniels' caller was the big boss, Brigadier General Billy Ford.

Sam had both of his dogs in the bathtub, their fur soaked and laden with soap when the phone rang. He decided to let the machine pick it up—until he heard Ford's voice.

"Sam? Are you there? Pick up the phone if you're there. We've got a situation in Zaire—it doesn't look good. Hemorrhagic fever, high mortality. Half a village bleeding and dying."

Daniels jumped to his feet. "Stay!" he ordered the dogs and then raced through the apartment and grabbed the phone. "Hi, Billy," said Daniels. "What's up?" Elsewhere in the Army it was unusual for a colonel to call a general by his first name—in USAM-RIID it was the norm.

"Looks like a bad one," said Ford grimly.

"How many dead?"

"Don't know. A lot." Ford was a highly educated and gifted doctor, a man of considerable taste and refinement. Sam Daniels could imagine Ford sitting behind his vast mahogany desk in his book-lined study, a serene, quiet room decorated with military antiques.

"Do we know what it is?"

"Looks like all the rest," said Ford with a sigh. "Lassa, Ebola . . . All I can tell you is that anyone who gets really sick, dies. I'm taking you off Hanta and flying you to Zaire."

Sam nodded. "Okay. I'll get my team together and get back to you . . ." He hung up and then realized that a quarter of his team was missing.

The dogs had not obeyed him and stayed in the bathtub. He discovered them lounging on his sofa, wet fur soaking into the material.

"I can't believe this!" Sam stopped and gaped. "You're wet, right? You guys are wet!

Which one of you disobeyed me first? Louis
. . . it was *you*, wasn't it." The dogs looking
away guiltily. Then it occurred to him—he
had a problem. Not only did he not have a
team, what was he going to do with the dogs?

Daniels was used to quick getaways. Well
before his departure time he was packed and
ready to go—the only matter still to be settled was housing his dogs. It was too late to
get them into a kennel and his new neighbors
were complete strangers to him, which left
him with a single recourse. . . .

When Robby opened her front door, her
guard was down and it stayed down long
enough for Sam to see that she was surprised
and pleased to see him. But her look hard-
ened in an instant and she turned away from
her ex-husband, lavishing her attention on
the dogs, who were delighted to see her.

"Hey, guys," she said. "I've missed you.
Come here and give me a kiss. I haven't seen
you in so long." Over her shoulder she spoke
to Sam. "You here to get the rest of your
stuff?"

Sam cleared his throat, feeling awkward and uncomfortable at Robby's cold reception.

"I've got to go away," he said.

"Where?"

"Zaire," he said. "Some cases of hemorrhagic fever. Not sure what it is."

"Casey going?" she asked. Robby felt a stab of jealousy. Fieldwork—dangerous though it might be—was the glamour side of the disease-killing business and there was a lot of it with USAMRIID. With a sizable budget and the resources of the U.S. Army at its disposal, there was a lot more travel with that outfit than with the Center for Disease Control.

"Yeah," said Sam. "And Jaffe I think. The whole crew." He smiled crookedly. "Most of it, anyway."

"And you want me to take the dogs," she said with a sigh.

"It'll just be four days."

"I'm flying to Atlanta on Friday," Robby said sternly. "If you're late, the dogs come with me."

Sam nodded. "Fair enough."

"I mean it."

"I know . . . So, what'll you be doing at CDC?" He did his best to keep his voice light, his tone conversational.

"Working in BL-4. Same as you."

"Who's supervising?"

"I am. Same as you."

"My job . . ." he said softly.

"I like to think of it as my job," she shot back. "Except I won't have the Pentagon breathing down my neck."

Sam was in no mood for confrontation. He picked up a mug on the kitchen counter and examined it. "This is mine," he said.

"I don't know," said Robby, shrugging. "Take it, and the rest of your stuff is in boxes over there. I'll hang on to it until you get back or I can just throw it away. Whatever."

Sam peered into the boxes that were stacked in the corner of the kitchen. He pulled a picture out of the top box and looked at it. It was a picture of the two of them, both clad in khaki field gear, standing in the middle of a tangle of jungle vegetation.

"You're giving me all the pictures of us?"

"Yeah," said Robby coldly. "Take them. You keep them."

"*You* keep them." He tossed the picture back into the box and headed for the door.

"I don't want them," she said, following him.

He opened the door and turned to her. "Me neither."

"Thursday, Sam," she said. "I mean it."

2

Dover Air Force Base
Dover, Delaware

AUGUST 20, 1995

By the time Sam Daniels got to Dover Air
Force Base, the skies had become overcast
and a light drizzle was falling, dispiriting
weather that matched his mood. He had been
unprepared for Robby's coolness or for the
effect that the sight of the house—*his* house—
would have on him. But there was little he
could do to dispel these blues, except, of
course, throw himself even deeper into his

work. The trip to Zaire had come along at precisely the right time.

The C-130 transport plane was sitting on the airport hardstand, the nose cone loading door open wide, exposing the vast cargo chamber. Dozens of soldiers were laboring to get the plane packed and prepped for a quick takeoff. The flight of tiny OH-6 Loach helicopters had already been loaded and dollies piled high with drugs and other supplies were being stowed.

In the middle of all the frenzied activity stood Major Conrad "Casey" Schuler. He was a doctor as well, had functioned as Daniels' right-hand man on a dozen trips into hot zones and had the distinction of being one of the least military-looking soldiers in the United States Army—though he made up for his lack of military bearing by being a dynamic and fearless disease fighter.

Schuler was also an old hand at loading airplanes. "Plasma goes in the reefer near the right wing. Gun it, guys, let's go. Gun it. Gun it. Gun it!" He looked critically at two soldiers inching a dolly and pallet up the ramp.

"C'mon, gun it!" Schuler ordered. "We're

late. Go, go, go, go, go!" He threw his own weight behind the load and shoved it into the plane.

Sam Daniels climbed down from the cockpit of the plane, saw Casey, and grinned. It was unusual to see senior officers engaged in manual labor. "Hey, Casey. Where's Jaffe?"

"Not making this trip. His wife just went into labor. I put him on leave."

"Who's going to read the tissue samples?" Daniels asked.

"You don't trust me."

"I do . . . But give me an alternative." This was bad news. Daniels had trained each member of his team personally and while he would be the first to admit that Schuler had irreplaceable skills, blood work and tissue samples were not among them.

"All right," said Schuler, "if you want the hot shot scope jockey out of Walter Reed you can have him, but frankly I'm hurt."

Sam Daniels was taken aback. This whole operation had been put together that morning, the chances of getting a replacement in such short order was almost impossible. "Just like that? Who cut his orders."

"The Old Man himself." He pointed across the tarmac.

General Ford was standing next to his parked Humm-Vee, directing a crowd of soldiers. Daniels walked over to Ford and saluted like the spit-and-polish soldier he wasn't.

"Hello, Sam," said Ford, returning the salute. "I thought maybe if I flashed my star out here, it might speed things up for you guys."

"Is it working?"

"No . . ." Ford pulled a large manila envelope from the Hummer and handed it to Daniels. "Personnel file on your new man. Also map coordinates, all the telex traffic so far and satellite photos from the last bird over Zaire."

Daniels pulled a sheaf of grainy ten-by-twelve enlargements protected by a clear plastic sleeve. There were eight black-and-white aerial views of an African village. Even taken from such altitude, Sam Daniels could see that the village was eerily deserted, with none of the marketplace bustle that he associated with African village life. A few of the huts had been set on fire, columns of dark smoke rising into the sky. The open ground was dotted with prone figures, as if they had died in their tracks, each corpse circled with a heavy grease pencil.

The two men exchanged grim looks. "Get in and out fast," said Ford. "As much as I dislike having you around here to make my life miserable, I don't want to lose you to some bug in the field."

"One question, sir. What have I ever done to make your life miserable?"

Ford laughed. "You got up this morning, didn't you?"

"Yes, sir. Thank you, sir."

"Good." They shook hands solemnly. "Now get going."

They were two hours into the flight, far out over the ocean, and Casey Schuler was in his trans-Atlantic mode. His shoes were off, feet up and sprawled across two seats, taking up a lot of room in the limited space allotted to passengers in the C-130. At his best, he never looked much like a soldier, but with Walkman headphones clamped over his ears, half a Snickers bar in his mouth, and his eyes glued to a copy of *Rolling Stone*, he was distinctly unmilitary-looking.

The contrast between Schuler and the new member of the team, Major Walter Salt, was startling. Salt was in his late twenties—young for a major—black, trim, and wore a crisp, well-cut uniform. He was doing his best to hide his shock and surprise at this senior officer's sloppiness. Salt was a graduate of West Point and in the Academy the first thing you learned was that neatness *counts*.

As Daniels came down the aisle from the flight deck, Salt sprung to his feet and saluted smartly. He held his shoulders taut and looked past Daniels, fixing his eyes on some point in the middle distance, in the approved military manner.

"Colonel Daniels, sir!" he barked, as if he were on the parade ground. "May I say what a privilege it is to have this opportunity to serve with you in the field."

"Thank you. Sit down, Major."

Salt looked a little confused by this, but an order was an order. Salt sat.

Daniels glanced at Casey, who gave a "Can you believe this guy" shrug.

"I have your service record," said Daniels, waving a dun-colored folder at the young major. "Your background is first-rate. Engineering degree from West Point, Johns Hopkins Medical School . . . You married?"

"Yes, sir."

"Good luck . . ." Sam scanned the folder. "Even did helicopter flight school, I see."

"Eighty-five hours logged, sir."

"But you've never been in the field."

Salt expected this would come up. "No, sir. But I'm fully trained—and highly motivated . . ."

Sam shook his head. "No, no, no, no . . . I'm talking about landing in a hot zone. It's a unique situation. Have you ever seen the effects of hemorrhagic fever on a human being?"

"No, sir."

Casey had finished his candy bar and had slipped off his headphones. He was following the conversation closely. "Allow me, sir," he said, his eyes bright. "Major Salt . . ."

"Yes, sir, Major."

"When the patient first gets the virus, he complains about flulike symptoms. In two or three days, pink lesions begin to appear all over his body, along with small pustules, which soon erupt, oozing pus and blood—a milky substance . . ."

Salt knew that Casey was trying to spook him, but he refused to be unnerved. He nodded and picked up the spiel. "The petechial lesions become fullblown, feel like mush to the touch. You vomit, get diarrhea, you bleed from the nose, gums, ears, your eyes begin to hemorrhage. Your internal organs shut down, liquefy. You're lucky if you go into a coma, sir . . . Major sir."

"Very good," said Sam. "We've all read the book. But you are about to see it."

"In the flesh," Casey put in. "So to speak . . ."

"I feel confident that I can handle anything we encounter, sir."

Sam shrugged. "Okay. It's just that . . . One of us panics, he puts us all in danger."

"And he's got direct orders not to die out there," said Casey. "And that's one set of

orders he's actually planning on following."
Salt didn't know it yet, but Sam Daniels
was not terribly good at following orders to
the letter.

"Is that clear, Major Salt?" Daniels asked.

"Yes, sir. I apologize, sir."

3

Motaba River Valley

The two OH-6 Loach helicopters darted in low and fast, flying no more than a hundred feet above treetop height, the jungle canopy streaking by beneath the skids of the aircraft like waves in a wide green sea. For a moment the vastness of the jungle was split by the broad brown breadth of the Motaba River snaking away for miles, then they were back over jungle.

The lead chopper carried Daniels and his

team, the second was packed with medical supplies. They were low enough that they could smell the land below them, the rich, loamy smell of Africa.

Salt took a deep breath of the lush scent as Casey fitted a clear Plexiglas helmet over his head, locking it down securely to the collar of his lightweight Racal biosafety suit. Casey and Daniels were wearing them also and moved easily in the stiff folds, and Salt did his best to look cool, but he felt claustrophobic and edgy.

"Checking respirator function." All of the suits were linked by radio and Casey's voice sounded tinny and hollow in the tiny speakers built into the suit.

He flipped a switch on Salt's portable respirator pack and the suit started to swell.

"Positive pressure's what you want," Casey explained. "Keep those little poisonous disease suckers out. Watch out for branches, thorns . . . someone passing you a joint— anything that could puncture or harm this suit. Okay?"

Salt nodded and tried to smile, but Casey could see that his face was already beaded with sweat. Even though now Casey Schuler wore his Racal suit like a pair of old blue jeans, he knew exactly what Salt was going through—he had felt the same way the first time he put on one of the cumbersome suits.

Daniels was seated up front, where the copilot would normally sit. He tapped the pilot on the shoulder.

"We've got a lot of supplies. You're gonna have to get us close."

The pilot, a burly master sergeant, licked his lips and shot Daniels a worried glance. "I sure wish I had one of them outfits, sir."

"You don't need one," said Daniels. "You'll be out of the zone."

"I—I don't want to get a disease, sir."

"Then don't kiss me, Sergeant."

The instant they touched down, Daniels was out of the cabin and on the ground, crouching under the whirling rotor blades. Casey patted Salt on the shoulder, a reassuring tap that said, "You'll do fine," then hopped out of the helicopter. Salt followed.

The heat, the smoke and dust, the cumbersome suits, and the aluminum equipment cases each man carried made traveling hard-going. Once the three men had cleared the billowing clouds of dust, the degree of devastation in the village became abundantly, horribly clear. It was an appalling sight, a vision of hell on Earth. The air was filled with the smoke from the burning huts, the crackling sound of the flames loud enough to be heard over the whine of the helicopter engines winding down. Clothes and household goods were scattered everywhere, as if dropped in panic. Here and there lay dusty human corpses, the flesh bloated by the sun and by the disease, looking as if ready to burst.

It was without a doubt the worst disease zone Daniels had ever been in. He looked behind him, looking to Salt to see how he was taking it. The young man had stopped and was looking down at the remains of a child, swollen like a distended doll. Casey saw Salt too and took him by the arm, moving him along. Virologists had to learn not to take each tragedy personally. It was the fastest way Schuler knew to make a mistake, to get sloppy, or to drive yourself insane.

They were making their way toward a rundown cinderblock building in the middle of the settlement, the village infirmary. Inside they found a lone doctor and two harried nurses tending dozens of patients, each stretched on a dirty pallet, mosquito netting hanging above the beds like shrouds. You did not have to have a lot of medical training to realize that each one of them was close to death.

"Dr. Iwabi?" said Daniels.

Iwabi and his small staff looked at the bizarrely equipped interlopers as if they were from another planet. It took a moment for Iwabi to find his voice.

"I am Benjamin Iwabi, yes. From the Zaire Infectious Diseases Health Agency, in Kinshasa." He was a short, slender man in his late forties and his eyes behind his wire-framed glasses were tired and streaked with red. The rest of his face was obscured by a surgical mask. "Are you Colonel Daniels?"

Sam nodded. "That's right. I brought antibiotics, plasma, antiserum—"

Iwabi shrugged, seemingly indifferent to such largesse. "You're too late."

"I came as soon as I could," Daniels protested.

"It wouldn't have mattered when you

came. This one is different—worse than Lassa, worse even than Ebola. It strikes and kills so fast. In a matter of days or hours and it doesn't matter who. The young, the healthy, everybody."

The Lassa and Ebola virus outbreaks of the 1970's had been terrifying eruptions of devastating diseases, two of the worst viruses Daniels had ever encountered. If this new disease was worse than those, then they were in serious trouble.

"Do we know the incubation period?"

"No," said Iwabi. "But it kills in two, three days. Mortality is one hundred percent."

"Jesus," Daniels gasped. "Could an infected person have gotten out of the village?"

Iwabi shook his head. "If he did, he would be dead or dying in the jungle. It's fifty miles to the nearest village."

"Who was the index case?"

"A local boy. He worked for the white man building the road through to Kinshasa. He was sick when he returned and he drank from the village well. From there it spread to the entire community."

"How did he get it? Did you identify the carrier?"

Iwabi shook his head slowly. "No. When the boy arrived he was incoherent. Died two hours later." Iwabi shrugged as if it hardly mattered anymore. "Now there's nothing to do but clean up. You can go home. The village is dead."

Salt was walking along the row of cots. He stopped at one and pulled aside the mosquito netting to inspect the patient, but the patient was already a corpse. His eyes were wide open and blood red, his flesh speckled with hemorrhages, as if there were a pulpy mass trapped under his skin. Thick, syrupy blood oozed from his ears, his mouth, his nipples. Salt recoiled in horror, gasping for breath and feeling his gorge rising in his throat.

"I—I'm gonna be sick . . ."

He coughed and started to wretch. Reflexively clawing at the straps that held his helmet. He had to have some fresh air or he felt as if he would pass out.

"Keep your helmet on!" Daniels ordered. He *knew* bringing an amateur into a hot zone was a bad idea and he cursed himself for having gone along with it.

"I can't breathe!" yelped Salt, his voice filled with a rising panic.

"Listen to me, goddammit!"

But it was no good. Salt vomited, yellow-green bile splashing on the Plexiglas. He tore off the helmet and dashed outside. Then he doubled over and filled his lungs with smokey air.

"Oh, shit . . . Get him out of here!" Daniels ordered. "Isolate him, isolate him."

Iwabi shook his head. "You don't need to put him in isolation," he said.

"Why?"

"Whatever this is, it is not spread in the air."

"How do you know?"

"It's very simple. If it was spread through the air I would be dead. For many days now, we've been working with only these masks. You know as well as I that they can't keep out a particle as small as a virus."

Iwabi pulled down his mask and took a breath. It was a kind of unspoken challenge—a gauntlet thrown down by the defenseless Africans, a dare to the sophisticated Americans in their high tech body suits. Daniels looked back at Iwabi, hesitating for a long moment, then he reached down and turned off his respirator. Slowly he removed the helmet and held it by his side.

Iwabi smiled wearily. "Believe me, you are quite safe."

"I hope so . . ."

Iwabi beckoned to Daniels to follow him outside. Behind the infirmary Zairian health workers were engaged in the grisly task of dousing dead bodies with gasoline and then setting them on fire. The smoke that rose from the corpses was greasy and thick, the air filled with the smell of broiling meat. Daniels had seen a lot, but he had never seen that. He turned away, knowing that the sight would haunt him for years to come.

Life in any African bush settlement revolved around the common source of water, the village well. At the best of times, the water was likely to be polluted with a mishmash of contaminants, none of them likely to be life-threatening. But Iwabi was right. If a fatal virus had entered the communal well, then the ruin visited on the village could not have been avoided, no matter how all-encompassing the care the patients had received.

Sam Daniels knelt and opened his equipment case. Very carefully he drew a sample of the well water with a syringe and put it into a vial. "You're sure no one could have left the village carrying the disease?"

"No," said Iwabi. "This virus, thank God, kills too quickly for a long-range dispersal. It kills everything in its path."

Daniels stowed his water sample and snapped the case shut. "Well," he said, "not everything." Sam was looking into the distance.

Iwabi followed his gaze as Daniels looked up toward the rock outcropping that hung over the village. Standing there was a man. He was dressed in traditional African garb and his face was daubed with ceremonial paint. He wore a headdress of matted grasses and there were bands of amulets encircling his wrists and ankles.

"He's not sick. Who is he?"

"The local juju man, a witch doctor." Iwabi smiled sardonically.

"Why isn't he sick?"

"There's a reason he's considered a wise man," Iwabi said. "At the first outbreak he retreated to his cave and greeted his visitors with poison darts. He's been there for the whole week."

"Will he talk to me?"

"No. To me he talked," said Iwabi. "He believes that the gods were awakened from their sleep by the men cutting down the trees to build a road where no man should be. The gods got angry and this is their punishment."

"He might have a point," said Daniels.

Just before dawn, on the cusp of the night and the beginning of a new day, the jungle came alive. As the eastern edge of the sky began to glow with the first rays of the rising sun, all the diurnal animals of the jungle awoke and in a matter of minutes the air was filled with the thousands of sounds of the rain forest. Birds screamed, cicadas set up their monotonous clicking, monkeys shrieked, and somewhere deep in vegetation a family of forest elephants trumpeted—but the loudest sound in the jungle that morning was made by man.

The engines of the two Loach helicopters burst into life and like huge birds rose from the landing zone, ascending like wraiths through plumes of smoke from the still-burning village. Dr. Iwabi watched them go, Daniels waving from the door of the lead helicopter.

Iwabi was not alone in watching the choppers take off. From the depths of the forest the monkey—the host—watched as odd, noisy birds floated into the sky and flew away.

The C-130 was fueled and ready, waiting on the tarmac in Kinshasa, the crew anxious to get going—horrible infectious diseases aside, the capital of Zaire was a scary, inhospitable place. They were still loading the helicopters when the pilot started the engines. Daniels and his team were in the passenger compartment already compiling their report for General Ford, Casey Schuler typing into a laptop computer as Daniels dictated.

Salt sat a few seats away, silent and lost in his own melancholy thoughts. He was used to excelling in almost every situation and now he was acutely aware that he had panicked and failed. He was sure he was going to get bounced off the team, fired before he had demonstrated his value. Salt glanced over at Daniels, wondering when the colonel would get around to firing him.

"Alarmingly high fatality," Sam dictated to Schuler. "All localized within a three-mile radius. Incubation period: short, appears contained." Daniels leaned forward to look at the computer screen. "Alarmingly, Casey, you didn't put in alarmingly . . ."

"It's an adverb, Sam—lazy tool of a weak mind."

"No they aren't."

Casey shook his head and read off the screen as he typed. "Surrounding villages and hospitals are to be monitored indefinitely for any further indication of the virus. Period. Done."

"Indefinitely is an adverb, Shakespeare," said Daniels.

"Ooops," said Schuler.

Sam reached for the computer. "I want to add something to that report." He typed rapidly and in caps: "BILLY—THIS IS THE SCARIEST SON OF A BITCH I HAVE EVER SEEN. AND YOU KNOW I'VE SEEN A LOT. SAM."

He read the entire report through quickly then, satisfied, he returned the computer to Casey. "Fax it to General Ford's house right away."

"Right."

Daniels walked down the aisle and sat down in the seat next to Walter Salt. The young major did his best to rustle up a smile.

"Sorry, sir," he said with a shrug.

"It's all right."

But Salt's standards were no lower than Daniels'—he refused to allow himself to be consoled. "No! No. No. I've never seen anything like that before. And I put the team in danger."

Sam shrugged. "We're still here."

"I got scared, sir."

Daniels nodded. "Fear's got a bad rap. All you have to do is listen to it with a more careful ear, that's all—more often than not it will save your life."

"But I put the team in danger," he said. "I have a lot of trouble forgiving myself for that. It could have been a disaster, sir."

"Could have been, but it wasn't . . . We're all here, we made it. Look, think about what happened for a minute, mark it under experience and put it behind you."

Salt nodded, but didn't look convinced. The ax was going to fall and he was trying to steel himself.

"You know, when it comes to viruses like the one we've just met, running away is probably the smartest thing someone could do."

Walter Salt winced, hating to be reminded that he had turned tail and run the first time out. "That's what you say, but you didn't run away."

"No," said Daniels evenly, "but I was scared shitless, just like you."

But Salt refused to go easy on himself. "But you could control it, sir."

Daniels sighed and tried approaching the

question from another angle. "Look, Salt, I don't want anyone working with me who *isn't* scared."

Salt's face lit up. "Well, sir, if that's the case . . . I'm your man." In spite of everything Daniels was going to give him a second chance—he wasn't going to get fired after all. He could hardly believe his luck.

Within twenty-four hours of the team's departure, the last patient in Iwabi's clinic had died and been incinerated. The village was abandoned by man and animals alike.

A small group of colobus monkeys were making a long circuit, a tour of their territorial domain. The family played and gamboled as they made their way down the path, unaware that one of their number was walking straight into danger. Crossing a ring of leaves, the monkey in the lead suddenly screamed in alarm—her hind foot snagged in a snare, then a net sprung, catching the beast and hanging upside down in the air. Hanging, swaying, the desperate animal shrieked in fear and pain, struggling to claw her way out of the all-encompassing net. But she could not escape. The host of the virus had been trapped . . .

4

Daniels always felt that there was something disorienting about transcontinental travel. It was faintly bewildering to spend several days in the interior of the African rain forest and then, twenty-four hours later, to find yourself at a cocktail party in a house on the Maryland shore.

He hadn't meant to crash General Ford's party, but he had gone directly there from the airport, still dressed in his wrinkled battle dress, determined to get Ford to issue an alert warning of the new virus.

But Ford refused to be unduly alarmed.

"Look, Sam, be reasonable . . . I can't write a memo that says the sky is falling. You said it yourself, the virus was contained in that village . . ." The general sipped his beer, then added, "It *was* contained, right?"

"I said containment was probable," Daniels corrected. "I still think we need an alert."

Ford held up his hand, like a cop stopping traffic. "Sam, do you remember back in '89? Two lousy cases of Congo fever in Nairobi and we had a note in every American kid's lunch box."

Daniels refused to be dissuaded. "I was wrong about that—"

Ford frowned then looked over at his guests, just to make sure the party was still going on without him. Then he turned back to Daniels, nodding vigorously. "That's right, Sam. You were wrong in '89. What about Lassa fever in '92?"

"I was wrong."

"Wrong again. But you're right about this?"

Sam shook his head. "No. I could be wrong about this too."

Daniels pushed a little harder. "This is a

level four virus. It doesn't get any worse than this. We have to be ready for it. We have to have an alert."

Ford was used to indulging his subordinate, but now he was getting a little annoyed. "You come waltzing into my party, smelling like dirty socks, snatch me away from Senator Rosales, whom I need not remind you, is chairman of the Senate Armed Services Subcommittee which is in charge of our budget."

"Forget Lassa or Ebola!" Sam Daniels' small measure of patience had run out. "This bug kills so fast you could die within—"

"Keep your voice down," Ford ordered curtly. Guests were casting curious glances in their direction. As if leading by example, Ford's own voice dropped to a whisper. "That's exactly my point. The very lethality of this virus is working for us. These unfortunate people don't live long enough to pass the virus around. So you're right. It *is* contained."

Someone came up behind General Ford and draped an arm around his shoulders. "Hell of a bash, Billy . . ." He was a tall, silver-haired man and he was smiling and attempting to be jovial, but the warmth didn't transform his eyes, which were pale and stern. He thrust a hand at Sam Daniels. "I'm afraid we haven't met, Colonel. General McClintock."

Sam shook his hand. "General." The men appraised each other. It was plain that McClintock had heard of Daniels; Daniels had never heard of McClintock, but he had met plenty of spooks in his time and he looked like one.

"Colonel Daniels was just telling me how refreshing a shower would be just now."

Daniels was dismissed. "Good to meet you, sir."

McClintock nodded graciously and watched as Sam threaded his way through the crowd and out of the house.

"If it's what I think it is," Ford whispered, "he brought it back."

"Safely?"

"Safely."

McClintock looked unperturbed. "And what did you tell him?"

"No more than he needs to know," said General Ford.

It was going to be a day of frustrations for Sam Daniels. After leaving Ford, he drove directly to Robby's house to reclaim his dogs.

"You were late," she insisted. "They're coming with me, just like we agreed."

He had arrived just as she was getting ready to leave. A taxi was waiting at the curb and her luggage was piled by the front door. Robby frowned when she opened the door to him, but the dogs seemed glad to see him. Much as he hated to do it, he gave her a hand, lugging her heavy suitcases out of the house and down to the taxicab.

"Come on, Robby—they're my dogs too."

"You never understood the concept of real time," said Robby. "What day is it?"

"Sunday," said Sam.

"When did you say you'd be back?"

"Friday."

"Thursday, Sam—Thursday."

Sam nodded. "That's right. Thursday. I meant Thursday."

"Thursday, Friday—they're so close together, even I confuse them." She picked up a suitcase and tried to jam it into the trunk of the cab. "Christ," she growled, "why didn't I just go to Atlanta when I said I would."

"Because you're a decent human being," said Sam. He tried to help her with the suitcase. "If you put the big pieces in first—"

Robby wrenched the suitcase away from him. She didn't want any more advice from him—she was sick of that, through with that.

"Fuck you, Sam. You were going to be home Thursday, I was going to fly Friday and see my new apartment . . . I'd go to my new job on Saturday, meet my new staff, buy a new toaster . . . Maybe have Sunday to rest . . ." The last of the luggage was crammed into the trunk. She slammed it closed savagely.

"Now I'm rushing to make my Sunday flight, I won't get to the apartment until seven; if I'm lucky I can buy the toaster but it will be nine before I have a chance to unpack . . . No, I can't unpack, because I have a nine o'clock hello-how-do-you-do staff party . . ." She pulled open the door of the back seat. Both dogs were lazing there happily, leaving only the tiniest sliver of room for her.

"Louis! Move over, move over."

"You're scaring him," said Sam. "Louis—"

The dog moved immediately. Robby looked angrily at Sam, annoyed that he had such control over the dogs. "That's because you let them on the couch," she said, climbing into the cab. She tapped the driver on the shoulder. "Okay. Let's go."

"Wait," said Sam. "How long are you keeping the dogs?"

"They are going with me, Sam. To Atlanta."

"They're my dogs too," he said. "I'll miss 'em."

Robby sighed heavily and shook her head. "Do you want the dogs, Sam? Either they go with me or they stay here with you. We are not going to split them up and we are not going to share them. You decide."

Sam couldn't respond. He wanted the dogs, but he didn't want to annoy Robby any more than he had already. Most of all, he didn't want her to go. . . .

But she was adamant. She snatched at the door handle and started to open the door. "Okay, you take them."

Sam shook his head and closed the door gently. "No, you keep 'em."

"Okay," she said. "Let's go."

"Wait! Wait a second. There's something I've got to say. Now I'm forgetting . . ." He searched his mind, trying to think of something, *anything* to delay her departure.

"Sam—I can't miss this plane."

"No, right, I remember now . . . When you go to the pet store, remember they like those medium-sized bones—"

"—barbecue flavored," said Robby impatiently. "I know, I know." But suddenly her anger was gone and now she really looked at her ex-husband. He seemed exhausted and helpless and Robby knew him well enough to know that it was more than the custody of the dogs—or even her departure—that was bothering him.

"You look tired . . . It was bad in Zaire, wasn't it?"

"Could have been better," he said with a shrug.

"What's the mortality?"

"About the same as our relationship," he said bitterly.

"You be careful," she said softly.

"I will . . . Good luck in Atlanta."

Sam stood and watched the car drive away, the dogs looking back through the rear window, as if saying goodbye . . .

The dogs were gone, Robby was gone, all that remained in his life was work. Sam Daniels fought jet lag all night and got to the lab the next morning bright and early.

He passed through the various security checkpoints, returning the salutes of the sentries. Sam Daniels approached the last set of metal doors before the BL-4 lab entrance and slipped his ID card into an optical reader. Almost instantly, the computer screen set in the wall printed out his name and serial number and a digitized voice boomed from the wall speaker.

"How-are-you-today-Colonel-Daniels?"

"Bursting with joy," said Daniels sourly. "And you?"

Sam's voice print appeared on the computer screen and it took only a second for the computer to match his voice against the example stored in the computer's memory. The doors clicked open and Daniels swept down the corridor, anxious to get to work.

He caught up with Casey Schuler in the central corridor leading to the labs. "Robby's gone. She left for Atlanta. Can you believe it, she's joined the CDC."

"Sam, you always knew she was going. This can't be that much of a surprise."

"She took the dogs."

"No kidding. How did that happen?"

"She took the dogs and left me the photographs—all the photographs from our marriage." He shook his head. "Can you believe it?"

Casey stopped. "Wait, let me get this straight. You didn't want the photos, but you *did* want the dogs. That it?"

"You're missing the point, Casey . . ."

"Was there a photo of the dogs?" Casey

asked. " 'Cause if you'd taken that, all your problems would be solved."

"Forget it, Case," said Sam sourly. "I open my heart to you and you make jokes."

"I'm not making jokes."

"When we got the dogs we were together, they were *ours*."

"They were cute," said Casey.

"Now that we're not together—"

"They're still cute."

"They're still *ours*."

"Then the dogs are probably a case for the Supreme Court."

"Look, I'm just asking if you think I'm right or wrong."

Casey had heard enough. "We're about to look at the most deadly virus that either of us has ever encountered and I think your mind should be somewhere in the neighborhood."

"It is."

"No it isn't . . ." Casey stopped and faced Daniels and spoke carefully, as if laying out a rational, cogent argument. "Look, she's got a new job at CDC. Strike that—she's got your job at CDC. She's starting a new life. She's happy. Strike that—she's happier. She's not coming back. It's nobody's fault. Move on. It's over . . . And quite frankly, I'm tired of hearing about it."

Sam gaped at him, as if hearing all this for the first time. "What do you mean, it's over?"

"Well . . . I think a state-sanctioned divorce order, signed by both parties, is strong evidence that something was off."

"Did you talk to her?" Sam demanded. "Did she say it was off?"

They were in the locker room outside of BL-4 now, climbing into their scrubs and snapping the gloves on their hands.

"Sam, do you know how I've managed to remain friends with the two of you?" He stripped some tape from the roll and wrapped it around his wrists.

"How?"

"I don't have conversations like this."

"I'm not asking you take sides," said Sam, although he wouldn't have minded if Casey chose to commiserate with him. "She's not a mean person. I know she didn't take the dogs to be mean . . . I'm just asking your opinion."

He taped his own wrists and then grabbed one of the blue biosafety suits.

"I don't have an opinion," said Casey. He pulled a red air hose from the ceiling and fitted the nozzle into a valve in his suit and inflated it, a standard safety procedure. Every piece of clothing had to be tested in this manner, looking for minute cracks and tears that might compromise the security of the suit.

"Everybody has an opinion," said Sam, zipping into his own suit.

"What the hell do you think you're doing?"

Daniels looked blankly at Shuler. "What? What?"

"You forgot to test that suit, Sam." Casey fingered the material. "Look! It's torn."

Suddenly, both men were sweating. A momentary lapse, a second of forgetfulness, could mean death. It was out of character for an old pro like Sam Daniels to make a mistake like that, and, to Casey it was an indication of just how upset he was over the death of his marriage.

Casey pulled a length of tape from the roll and pressed it over the rent in the protective suit. "Hey, if you get cooked who've I got left to dump on?"

"Thanks, Case. Takes your breath away."

The air lock procedures for the BL-4 lab were elaborate and foolproof. Clad in their protective suits, Casey and Daniels got into the first chamber in the lock and plugged their suits into two long red cords which supplied air to their helmets. One side of the lock closed as the other opened, Casey and Daniels stepping into the lab proper, their air hoses—umbilical cords, as they were known around the lab—running on complex tracks set in the ceiling.

The laboratory was a large, brightly lit room dotted with equipment and work stations. In the center of the room were bulky circular freezers, each secured with a combination lock. It was in these stainless steel vats that thousands of different diseases slept, inert in dry ice.

There were no windows in the laboratory and no source of natural light. The only things on the walls were two large screens hooked up to the two electron microscopes and could be used for video projections.

The two men were surprised to discover that they were not the first in to work that morning. There was a third space-suited figure in the lab working under a pressure hood at an electron microscope.

Walter Salt emerged from under the hood. "Good morning, Colonel. I took the liberty of bringing in the Motaba samples myself."

Daniels was pleased with Salt's display of initiative. "Early riser, Casey." His tone of voice suggested that Schuler might learn something from Salt.

"Hey, I was up at four. Took a piss, went back to sleep."

"Salt, thaw a sample of the virus, separate it, and get it under the scope."

"Done," said Salt. "We'll have the results in a couple of hours."

Sam beamed. *"Very good,* Major Salt."

Casey strolled over to a stainless steel cart containing a rack of aluminum vials, picking up the one labeled Motaba No. 7. He tossed it lightly in his hands, playing with it.

"Motaba . . ." he said. "Listen to the way it rolls off your tongue. Mo-ta-ba . . . sounds like a perfume, doesn't it?"

Salt couldn't help but be alarmed. In spite of the high tech suits and the elaborate containment procedures, these diseases just weren't things that you played with. He glanced over at Daniels, expecting to see that he was just as horrified, but he wasn't, in fact, he seemed to be enjoying the moment. Casey did a little dance and rubbed the vial across his chest seductively, as if it really did contain perfume.

"Mo-ta-ba . . ." he said breathily. "One drop and you feel so . . . *different*. Your lover will melt in your arms. Here! Try a sample."

Without warning he tossed the vial to Salt. For a moment, time seemed to stand still, the container spiraled across the room, turning end over end. Salt felt a flash of fear and a moment of hesitation, but instinct won through—his hands went up and he caught the tube. But it wasn't the Motaba tube—it was a plain old glass test tube that Casey had snatched and thrown.

Casey nodded approvingly and waved the vial of Motaba at Salt. "Good hands, Salt . . . Not as quick as mine. Don't mess with this stuff. We're professionals. Gotta be ready for anything. Ain't nothing in here that can't kill you."

"Including the air," said Sam. "Now that we've initiated Major Salt . . . I need an eliza test and a PCR primer pair."

Casey was all business now, the hijinks of a few moments before forgotten. "We need a blood test for this yesterday."

"I'm already on it, sir," said Salt crisply.

"Yes, sir." Energized and happy, Salt returned to his microscope.

Daniels was far from finished dispensing orders, "Casey: live animal studies. I want tropism, antiviral responses, kill rates. Give me all possible vectors. Is this thing carried by an insect, a rodent, or what?"

"I'll freeze him, drown him, shake and bake him."

"Case . . . there's a good chance at seeing a virus no one has ever seen before."

Casey Schuler grinned. "That's why we do what we do in blue, Sam."

Salt looked up from his microscope. "Sirs, does that make me black and blue . . . ? Sorry, sirs."

"Salt! Where's my mug shot?"

"Yes, sir." Salt returned to the computer console attached to the electron microscope. "Yes, sir. Got it right here. We've compressed eight hours into thirty seconds and generated an enhanced computer image." He dimmed the lights in the room and then projected an image from the microscope onto one of the wall screens.

The culture of live human cells appeared from the haze of images, the circular discs bumping along the bloodstream like boats. Salt sharpened the focus slightly.

"Normal, healthy liver cells . . ." he said. "Okay, here comes trouble . . ." An infected cell appeared in the bloodstream. It is different from the others on the screen—this one was as black as a rotten tooth and weird snakelike forms wriggled within the cell, making the organism look as if it were trembling on the screen.

"Those snakes are the virus," Salt explained. "In the course of an hour a single virus has invaded the cell here, multiplied and killed it . . . Two hours and it's invaded nearby cells . . . and they continue to multiply."

The wriggling of the virus intensified, as if it were boiling within the cell until the membrane burst. The snakes streamed out of one host and into the bloodstream, slashing about, scores of them, hundreds, swarming onto the surfaces of the healthy cells with terrifying speed and rapacity. It was as if these things were actually hungry and needed to devour the healthy, living cells around them.

"Jesus Christ," said Casey. "Replicates, kills, reinvades this fast? These numbers can't be right. Ebola takes three days . . ."

"The numbers are correct, sir," said Salt. He raced forward to the conclusion of the example. The screen was almost black with the virus. "That's all she wrote for this culture. Every cell is dead. This murkiness . . . that's the virus . . . one has turned into millions." He increased the magnification. "The membrane of a single cell. The virus has replicated and turned the cell to mud. If one of them is grandad, then some of them are his grandkids. Looking to become grandaddies themselves. This family don't believe in weddings."

"But they sure as hell love large receptions," said Casey.

Salt flicked a switch on the console and the

magnification on the screen changed. "Closer . . . closer . . . closer . . . Here we go."

The images loomed larger and larger, the computer enhancement kicking into high gear. The fuzzy, snaking forms vanished. "Gentlemen," said Salt. "Meet Mr. Motaba."

The three scientists stared at the image, the light reflected on their face shields, making it look as if the virus were crawling across their skin, into their noses and eyes.

"I *hate* this bug," said Casey softly.

As Daniels stepped closer to the screen for a better look, Salt bumped the images up to the highest level of magnification. The virus seemed to loom over them like an evil spirit. Daniels looked with awe and fear, but also with determination, a conviction that he would take on this disease and destroy it.

"It's the perfect beast," said Sam. "It doesn't want to be here. We're the first to see it and now it's our job to destroy it."

At that moment, however, he did not look equal to the task, appearing puny compared to his foe. The virus looked cold, alien, almost mechanical-looking—and utterly deadly.

5

The moon had risen over the USAMRIID complex, the parking lot was almost empty and even enthusiastic, driven researchers like Salt and Schuler had thrown in the towel and gone home hours before. Sam Daniels was battling fatigue himself and realizing that the longer he stayed the smaller the returns would be. The time had come—he had to call it quits for the day and face the empty house.

But General Ford was still there. He watched a bank of security monitors, tracking Daniels' progress through the building, from the BL-4 lab to the locker room, then down the long corridor to the main exit. There were two sentries on duty there and they snapped to attention as he passed, Daniels giving them a weary salute.

Ford waited until he saw that Daniels had left the building, then stood and made his way toward the lab. A corporal stationed at one of the corridor checkpoints was surprised to see the Big Man himself, but it wasn't up to a noncom to ask a general why he was bothering to work late.

The general's salute was a little more spit and polish than Daniels' had been. "As you were, Corporal," the general said as he swept by. He looked a lot calmer and more confident than he actually felt, but he betrayed not a trace of nervousness.

Ford entered the locker room and slipped into his own suit of green surgical scrubs and then his blue biosafety suit. He walked through the air lock, tethering his umbilical cord to the air supply, then stepped into the lab itself, moving quickly across the big room. Suddenly, his air tube snagged on the sharp corner of a lab bench, stopping him in his tracks and threatening to pull from the suit. He stopped, frightened, quickly checking his hose. It was stretched and dented but not broken and it had held in its mooring in his suit, but it had been close. In this atmosphere—alone—any mistake could lead to sudden and immediate contamination.

Ford allowed himself to breathe again, relieved. "The world is *round,* you guys," he muttered. "Didn't anyone happen to mention that?"

He grabbed a metal file from one of the tool boards and rasped down the corner of the bench until it was perfectly smooth and rounded. The general was in a hurry—but there was always time for safety precautions in the BL-4 lab.

Once he had finished with the corner he walked across the lab to one of the circular freezers and punched a seven-digit entry code into the security keypad. The lock snapped open instantly and as he lifted the heavy lid heavy condensation vapor rose in a cloud. Inside the freezer, lying in metal racks were twelve aluminum tubes, each one labeled Motaba. Ford carefully removed one of them and resealed the chest.

Ford was not alone. Coming through the airlock were two men, their silver biosafety suits indicating that they were strangers to this facility. They did not say a word as they crossed the room, one of them taking the Motaba tube from Ford, the other opening a clear Plexiglas box and removing an identical vial within.

Ford nodded to the two men, as if giving them permission to proceed, and then left the lab, his part in the operation completed. As he passed through the air lock, though, he looked over his shoulder. The technicians were settled at one of the electron microscopes, silently going about their business. . . .

Only the gray glow of a blank video screen lit his office, the rest of the orderly, Spartan room was in darkness. With a heavy sigh, Ford sank into the high-backed leather chair behind his desk. He rubbed his eyes and temples, as if trying to massage away the headache that was beginning to pound through his brain.

He did not jump when a cigarette lighter flared in the corner of the room, the tiny eruption of flame illuminating the face for only a split second. That kind of sudden, dramatic gesture was McClintock all over—and Ford had grown used to that sort of thing dating back to the days when McClintock had been the leader and Ford had been nothing more than his aide.

"You look tired, Billy." Major General Donald McClintock was wreathed in smoke and his features were indistinct, but Ford could imagine the lean, gaunt face, the iron gray hair, the slightly condescending cast to his mouth.

"Colonel Daniels is not going to like our going behind his back like this."

"Then we'll kill him." McClintock laughed dryly. "C'mon, lighten up, Billy. We have no alternative. You're so goddamn sentimental. That's the trouble with this whole country . . . sentimenfuckingtality."

Ford looked at him sharply. To McClintock

life was a game to be played and won, no matter the human cost. Before he could say anything, though, Ford's telephone beeped softly. He picked up the handset, listened for a moment, then replaced it.

"They're ready."

"Good," said McClintock.

A haze of static clouded the video screen, then an image appeared on the left-hand side of the monitor. It was an attenuated viral, a DNA double helix, labeled "Motaba Valley, 1967." A moment passed and then a second, blurry image appeared on the right-hand side of the screen: another double helix, this one marked "Motaba Virus—Daniels—1995." Even a layman could see that the two specimens were identical. A disease that had vanished almost thirty years earlier had come back to life.

Even after all this time, Ford had never forgotten that terrible day. The grotesque tangle of that meaningless war, the mercenary camp, the doctor, the dead and dying, the terrified soldiers. The death and fire that McClintock had showered on them . . .

"Oh God . . . It's our old friend," said Ford. "Back for a hey hello."

"Son of a gun," said McClintock. "Daniels didn't find the host did he?"

"No."

McClintock turned from the video screen and looked at Ford, his eyes pale, icy, emotionless. "Lock it up, Billy. Shelve it. You know about this. I know about this. Nobody else. Get your friend Daniels off the case. I don't want that nosy little bastard messing up thirty years of national security work. You understand that?"

Sam Daniels found the orders on his desk when he came in the next morning. They were written in the cramped, lifeless language of army bureaucratese, but Sam caught the meaning instantly. It was nothing more than a single paragraph over General Ford's signature: Daniels and his team were being pulled off research on the Motaba virus.

He stared at it for a moment, rereading it

twice, then stalked down the hall. Daniels did not respect army protocol at the best of times—and this was far from the best of times. He pushed into Ford's office and slammed the door behind him. Ford was standing by his desk going over some papers with his secretary, Sergeant Dixon.

"What the hell is going on?" demanded Daniels.

Ford, as unflappable as always, looked at Daniels over his glasses. "Sergeant," he said softly, "would you be good enough to get us some coffee?"

"Sir," said Dixon. He exited as discreetly as a butler.

"Why are we being pulled off Motaba?"

"Calm down," said Ford sharply. "And don't you ever talk to me like that again in front of the troops. You know better than that."

Daniels did his best to control himself but it took all his strength. "Yes, sir."

Ford sighed and dropped his papers on his desk. "Sit down, Sam. I thought we agreed Motaba was contained."

"It's contained now," Daniels replied. "It's

gonna pop up later. We don't have a blood test yet. We don't know how it's transmitted. We don't know diddly squat."

"Sam," said Ford wearily. "There's a fresh outbreak of the Hanta virus in New Mexico. The CDC needs some help. I'm sending you."

"Send Petersen's team," said Sam curtly.

Ford's anger flashed. "Don't tell me who to send on assignment. I told Senator Rosales I'd send my best man. That's you. Now get out of here."

Daniels looked at the ceiling, rolling his eyes. "We've got baseline information on Hanta. What are you sending me out there to do? Trap rats? Billy, we've got the bug growing; most proteins isolated; we'll have an antibody test in a week . . ."

"Sam," said Ford, "I have given you your orders."

"For God's sake, Billy, listen—Casey has put the bug in rodents and rhesus. If all goes well, we'll know its genetic sequence in a month. If you leave us alone we'll map this guy down to the last gene . . . It'll make you famous."

Daniels' tenacity was beginning to bother

Ford. "Sam, the odds of Motaba causing us any more trouble are a million to one and you know it."

"No, I don't know that."

"Well, you should—and you would if you didn't harbor this morbid desire to face the end of the world. Now please!"

"This is the biggest thing we've ever seen."

"You're killing me," said Ford.

"It's a fresh, brand-new virus," said Sam Daniels desperately, a last-ditch effort to change Ford's mind.

But the general was unmoved. "You're still killing me. Now get out of here."

A curious air of mourning hung over the lab. Salt, Daniels, and Casey looked into the empty freezer as if it were a tomb.

"Every last sample of Motaba is gone," said Daniels. "Where the hell did they put it all?"

"General Ford ordered me to move all tubes to the sealed vault in A Wing," said Salt. "Only he has access there . . . He said we weren't gonna need 'em for several months."

"I can't believe that they're really doing

this," said Daniels. He turned to Casey. "Where are the primary specimens?"

"None," said Casey.

"There's nothing in the incubator? We can grow this back in no time—I'll tell them we're growing Hanta out of rat shit."

Sam Daniels looked to Casey, expecting support. Schuler positively enjoyed subverting authority—but he didn't look pleased now. In fact, he was hanging his head.

"Case . . . ?"

"I'm shocked," said Casey.

"What?"

"I'm shocked . . ." Casey looked up and grinned. "And ashamed of myself . . ."

Sam watched, puzzled, as Casey crossed the room and withdrew a tube from a freezer. "I am ashamed of myself because I carelessly misplaced one of the Motaba samples yesterday—and put it in here. I know that if I give this to you it will be in good hands and that you will make sure my mistake is corrected . . . sir."

The two men shared a conspiratorial smile.

Sam shook his head. "Always, always,

Casey, I am forced to deal with your care-lessness."

Schuler shrugged. "You know me . . ."

Aboard the Freighter
Tae Kuk Seattle

AT SEA, AUGUST 29, 1995

The Korean break-bulk freighter was plow-ing through heavy seas, ninety miles out, making for the port Oakland, California. It was carrying a varied cargo, electronics, and cheap clothing from South Korea, engine parts from Japan and a small menagerie of exotic animals that were consigned by an animal broker in Singapore. Some of the ani-mals were meant for American zoos and wild animal parks, but most, including a black-and-white colobus monkey were intended for labs and biological-testing facilities all over the country.

The animals were under the care of the

lowest-ranking seaman on the ship, a twenty-one-year-old seaman second class, named Chan Ho Lee. It was his first trip and he felt seasick and lonely, tired of the bullying and teasing of the more senior crew members. They thought they had been punishing him when they gave him the dirty and unpleasant job of taking care of the animals, but in actual fact the time he spent in the hold was the best part of his long working day. The animals were the only living creatures on board who were worse off than he was and they helped to pass the time and ease the pain of the passage.

He was particularly fond of the little black-and-white monkey. He made sure that he saved some small part of his meals to bring as a treat for her—some rice balls, perhaps, or a piece of fruit—and she seemed to appreciate it.

Yet, Seaman Chan could tell that she was not happy. Of course, he did not know that this was only the latest leg in a terrifying journey that had taken her from her home. After she had been captured the monkey had been carried down to Kinshasa and loaded onto a plane which took her to the Mozambique port of Maputo. There she had been packed into her tiny cage to begin a long sea voyage across the Indian Ocean to Jakarta and from there on to Singapore. She had been terrified for every minute of every day.

Chan pushed a piece of banana through the bars of the cage and the monkey snatched it, then retreated to the far corner, studying the young man with plaintive eyes. He tried to reach far enough in to stroke her dirty fur but he couldn't reach.

"What's the matter, girl?" he said softly. "Don't worry. This trip is almost over. You'll feel better soon . . ." Chan sighed. The monkey would be fine. *He* on the other hand had to endure the long return trip. . . .

BL-4 Lab
Frederick, Maryland

AUGUST 29, 1995

Casey Schuler took charge of the meager supply of Motaba and began to run tests. It didn't take him long to establish some basic facts about Motaba, none of them good. Late in the day, he and Salt led Daniels into the animal-testing section of the BL-4 lab, an underground warren lined with cages. Diseases were let loose in that chamber, so biosafety suits and air locks were essential here too.

Casey wasn't grinning anymore. "This bug definitely ate its Wheaties," he said.

Daniels stopped short. A pair of white rats lay dead in one cage. He looked around the room—there were dead animals in every test cage: guinea pigs, mice, hamsters, birds, rabbits. . . .

"Tell me what we know," said Daniels.

"It spreads through moisture," Salt explained. "That's body fluids or direct physical contact."

"That rules out an insect host and insect

transmission," said Schuler. "No test species survived and I've treated them with all known antivirals. I guess that's the good news—we're not looking for ticks, fleas, flies, mosquitoes, that sort of thing."

Daniels and Salt walked the length of the cages, looking at the dead animals. It was apparent through the fur and feathers that these creatures had died horrible deaths.

"What about airborne? Dust, wind . . ."

"Casey shook his head. "Negative. It dries out. Dr. Iwabi was right."

"Thank God for that," whispered Salt.

"Well, that's really the end of the good news. Once this guy hits tissue—the lethality is like nothing we've ever seen. Not one of the test species has survived, even when I've treated them with all known antivirals."

Daniels was incredulous. "Bullshit. You used intravenous acyclovir?" This powerful drug was the heaviest piece of hardware in the virus-fighting artillery.

"No effect," said Casey.

"Ribovirun?"

"Hey, you can *bathe* this guy in it," Casey scoffed. "He'll still bench-press the Sunday

Times." There was a note of admiration in Casey's voice. Motaba was a killer, but it was a challenger worthy of the contest.

"Jesus . . ."

"And it's smaller than we thought, Colonel," said Salt. "We were worried that we didn't have enough of the stuff . . . Millions of these can fit into a single drop of human blood."

"Enough to wipe out half the U.S. population," said Casey.

"Great," said Sam with a shrug. "This thing kills everything and we can't treat it."

"There's our challenge." Schuler had the tiniest smile on his face.

Daniels stepped closer to the rabbit cage and looked at the lifeless, blood-splattered corpses. They were twisted and contorted, their eyes terrified and opened wide as if they had seen their approaching death. In all his life, Daniels had never encountered such a fearful opponent and it frightened him more than he could say.

Center for Disease Control
Atlanta, Georgia

AUGUST 29, 1995

Dr. Roberta Keough was settling into her new life and it was a little more difficult than she had anticipated. There was a longstanding rivalry between the Center for Disease Control and the U.S. Army Infectious Diseases Division and there were those on the CDC staff who suspected that her sudden conversion to the cause was less than sincere. She did her best to reassure her new colleagues that despite her background she was on the team wholeheartedly. Nevertheless, she resented criticisms of her former colleagues, her husband included—she knew firsthand that the men and women at USAMRIID were extremely dedicated and highly skilled.

Solving the quandary was not made any easier by Sam Daniels. The first call she took that morning was from her ex-husband and she knew at once that something was up. Sam didn't open with any pleasantries, didn't ask about her new life, didn't even inquire after the welfare of the dogs.

"Robby," he said, his voice low and intense, "this call is unauthorized."

Robby blinked. "What are you saying? Are you telling me that this is outside of channels?"

"That's exactly what I'm saying."

"Are you out of your mind? You'll get drummed out of the service for sure." The Pentagon did not forgive members of the armed forces who bypassed official procedures and went to the civilian world.

"Rob, I need your help."

"Help with what?"

"Motaba. You know, the thing I went to Zaire for. This is the big one, Robby. This thing is death itself. If it gets into circulation in this country then we are well and truly cooked. And I mean that literally."

"What are you saying, Sam? If it is as bad as you say then Ford and the rest of the brass will be behind you every step of the way. There's no need to come to us—"

"That's the weird thing, Robby, Ford has dropped the ball. He's put a lock on Motaba—he won't even sanction research. The day before yesterday we could write our own ticket. As of this morning, we're supposed to be working on Hanta in New Mexico."

"People are dying of Hanta, Sam."

"Right, Hanta is out of the bottle. Motaba isn't yet. The deaths have been confined to a small part of Africa. This one is bad, Robby. It has all the hallmarks of a Class Four son of a bitch. Incredible fevers, petechial lesions . . . If it gets loose . . ." She could hear him sigh and could imagine the intense look on his face. "We have to be on the lookout for it. I need the CDC to put out a bulletin. Now."

There was a long silence.

"Are you listening to me?" Sam asked.

"Yes," said Robby. "I'm listening."

"Are you writing this down?"

"I wrote it down."

"So you'll send out the alert?"

Robby shook her head. "No," she said curtly. "I am not going to base one of my first official decisions on a hunch when the Army won't even back you."

"Hunch? Robby—I'm faxing you the whole epidemic. I've got a lab full of dead animals! No response to intravenous acyclovir, to riboviral. They're all dead."

There was real desperation in his voice, but Robby refused to be swayed. "Of course they're dead," she snapped. "You stuck 'em all with the same needle. Where's the evidence that it's coming here?"

"There's no evidence that it won't," said Sam. "I'm telling you I've got a bad feeling."

"Okay, Sam," said Robby, "your feeling is in my notes."

Daniels was in no mood for further argument. "There's nothing complicated about this. It's very simple: this thing kills everything in its path. Just tell them to put out the alert. Do it."

"This is beginning to sound familiar," said Robby archly. "Is that an order, Colonel Daniels?"

She could hear him sigh in exasperation. "I can't believe you're turning a deadly virus into a family matter."

"It's not personal, Sam."

But it *was* personal—at least it was to Sam Daniels. "Robby, why don't you take one fucking chance for once in your life."

"I did," she snapped back. "I married you." Then she hung up on him.

Biotest Animal Holding Facility
San Jose, California

AUGUST 30, 1995

The monkey's journey was far from over. The *Tae Kuk Seattle* was off-loaded in San Francisco, but the monkey's destination was San Jose, forty-four miles to the south at the head of San Francisco Bay. Her cage was pulled out of the hold, swung into blinding daylight, then locked in the pitch black of a tractor trailer for the long, noisy ride.

When the rear doors of the truck finally opened, the cage was taken off the truck and put on a forklift and trundled into a vast warehouse. Inside were cages stacked three high—each one contained a monkey, but the new arrival was the only colobus, the rest being brown rhesus monkeys. The close, fetid air of the warehouse was filled with the screams and shrieks of terrified animals.

The forklift operator found the space allotted for the colobus and stacked the cage. He poked his fingers through the cage, touching the animal.

"Hey, babe, I'm Jimbo." He was a tall,

rather scrawny guy with scraggly black hair that fell to his shoulders. When he smiled he showed a mouthful of uneven teeth.

Jimbo Scott rattled the cage, pounding out a quick percussion beat. Just then the beeper clipped to his belt sounded. He turned it off and looked at the return number glowing red in the LED display. It was a number Jimbo was always happy to see because it always meant a little extra money.

Jimbo looked at the monkey and winked as the monkey wailed and whimpered. "It's okay, girl. We're all creatures of God here, right? And you'll be out of this place quick smart, I promise . . ." He swung up into the seat of the forklift again. "Catch you later."

In Jimbo Scott's mind, the job at the Biotest warehouse was temporary—extremely temporary—because Jimbo had big plans. He was a drummer in a rock and roll band and Jimbo thought it was just a matter of time before the big break came. Until opportunity in the form of megastardom came calling, however, Jimbo was always on the lookout to make a little spare cash. The job with Biotest paid poorly and Jimbo's needs were great. He augmented his income any way he could.

Jimbo had an arrangement with a pet shop in Cedar Creek, the proprietor of which had a small sideline in exotic animals. Jimbo stole animals from Biotest to order—and it just so happened that an order for a female colobus monkey had just come in.

He left work at five that afternoon but he was back by six knowing that the warehouse would be deserted by then. The only human being on the site would be the night watchman, a young man named Neal who, Jimbo knew from experience, was never averse to making a little easy money.

Neal smiled conspiratorially when Jimbo drove his battered Volvo up to the gate. He could see that there was a cage covered by a blanket in the back seat.

"So your ship came in again, eh, Jimbo?"

Jimbo already had two twenty-dollar bills ready. He handed them to Neal and winked. "That's our ship, Neal, our ship. Yeah?"

"I hear ya."

"Ship just come in from Africa. A land of great beauty and untold riches."

Neal stuffed the bills into his trouser pockets. "Absolutely untold."

"Gonna transact a little business," said Jimbo. "Then I'm outta here."

"Where you going?"

"Vacation. Going to Boston to see my girl."

Neal punched a button in the guardhouse control panel and the gate swung open. "Have a good trip."

"See you on the way out."

The whole thing was so simple. All Jimbo had to do was let himself into the warehouse, grab the monkey, and put her in the cage he had brought, as an afterthought he tossed in a plastic baby bottle full of water and half a banana.

"There you go. Don't say I never give you nothing." The monkey bared her teeth and lashed out with her claws. Jimbo hardly flinched. He was used to working with animals, so the creature's spits and scratches hardly slowed him down. The most complicated part of the theft was logging on to the warehouse computer and removing the colobus from the inventory, and that only took a minute or two.

Jimbo waved to Neal as he drove off the lot and was soon heading north on Route 680, making good time for Cedar Creek, the radio blasting.

The colobus was not happy. She chattered and jumped nervously in her cage, the blaring music and the speed at which they were traveling making her agitated and jittery. Jimbo hardly noticed. He was by nature a happy-go-lucky young man, not given to introspection or soul-searching; his theft didn't bother him in the slightest. All he was interested in doing was getting his money and then flying off to Boston. Life, generally, was good. . . .

Jimbo pounded the wheel in beat with the music, watching the monkey in the rear-view mirror. He half turned in the driver seat and winked at the animal.

"What's the matter, baby? Music is supposed to soothe the savage beast."

The monkey sucked a mouthful of water from the bottle and spat at Jimbo. Her aim was perfect, hitting him square in the face, drenching him with water and saliva.

"Little shit!" Jimbo wiped his face, surprised and angry that the monkey had nailed him so unerringly. "Lucky for you I don't have a Michael Bolton tape for punishment . . ."

The rest of the trip was uneventful. By the time he arrived at his destination Jimbo had forgotten all about his little tiff with the monkey.

Center for Disease Control
Atlanta, Georgia

AUGUST 30, 1995

Robby Keough could not stop thinking about the conversation with her ex-husband. He was headstrong, he was infuriating—but he was also smart. And there was no doubt in her mind that Sam had sounded worried, but it wasn't the first time he had sounded an alarm bell unnecessarily. It was, however, the first time he had flouted USAMRIID convention and gone outside of the department channels. She knew Sam was unpredictable, a loose cannon, but not even he would take a step so serious without good reason.

Robby snatched up some papers lying on her desk and attempted to do some work, but she couldn't concentrate, her eyes refusing to focus on the words printed on the page in front of her. She stared angrily at the phone, half expecting it to ring, Sam calling again with another barrage of extremely persuasive arguments.

Then she said, aloud, "The hell with it." She gathered up the notes she had taken during her brief conversation with Sam and marched down the hall to the office of the director.

She had met Dr. Drew Reynolds twice. Once when she had been interviewed for the job and once again when he gave her the traditional "Welcome aboard" speech. Beyond that she found this man remote and austere, an intimidating presence in his trademark seersucker jacket and Waspy bow tie.

She knocked on his door and peered around the frame, hoping that he wasn't in a meeting. "Excuse me, Dr. Reynolds . . ."

Reynolds, typing furiously at his computer console, glanced at her and held up one hand while typing with the other. "One moment," he said and went on typing for a full minute before stopping, examining his words on the screen and turning to his newest recruit.

"What can I do for you, Dr. Keough?"

"Um . . . Dr. Daniels up at USAMRIID wants us to send out a special bulletin warning all physicians to watch out for symptoms of a virus from Zaire called Motaba. He thinks it serious enough that it can't wait for our regular monthly report." Her words came out in a rush, as if she said it fast enough he wouldn't focus on their exact meaning.

Reynolds regarded her over the tops of his half-frame glasses, looking at her as if he had suddenly been confronted with the realization that he had somehow hired a half-wit.

"A special report?"

"That's right."

"The warning will be included in our weekly report, Dr. Keough," Reynolds said curtly.

Robby felt she had to press the point. "That doesn't go out until next Wednesday. Colonel Daniels believes this is serious enough to send out an immediate alert. And I think he has a point."

Dr. Reynolds whipped his glasses off his nose and twirled them. He was smiling and there was something about that gesture that unnerved her. "Do you know what it costs to send out a special alert to four hundred thousand health officials?"

"Is that my job?"

"No," said Reynolds. "It's my job."

"In '89 he predicted Hanta and it hit," said Robby.

"I suppose I understand your allegiance to your ex-husband, but we hired you, not him. And you know as well as I do that the chances of this virus showing up in the U.S. are virtually nil. Am I right?"

The two locked eyes for a moment.

"That's your call, Dr. Reynolds."

Reynolds nodded. "I know. The warning will be included in our weekly report."

Keough was dismissed. Her cheeks burning, she turned and walked out of the office. She did not see the sour look that Reynolds shot after her, which was just as well because Robby was feeling as low as she had in months.

She managed to keep her composure all the way to the elevator. Once inside though, she slumped against the wall, close to tears. Life was not working out quite the way she had hoped and she still felt the pull of her broken marriage.

People were waiting for the elevator on the landing of her floor, so Robby was forced to pull herself together, reassuming, through considerable effort, a confident and professional manner. Like Sam Daniels, she knew only one way out of the blues: more work.

6

Cedar Creek, California

SEPTEMBER 1, 1995

Cedar Creek was a small town on Route 101 north of Sonoma, a quiet community of only a few thousand inhabitants, its size limited by geography. It was too far from San Francisco to attract a commuting population—farming and wine-making were the primary occupations here.

Rudy Alvarez owned the only pet shop in the town and for most of his career he had maintained a perfectly ordinary store. He sold puppies and kittens, the occasional bird, and a lot of pet food. He had gotten into dealing in exotic animals gradually but had come to appreciate the money they brought in. A single monkey could earn as much as a litter of pedigree puppies, particularly if he got it hot and cheap from Jimbo Scott.

But there were risks associated with unusual animals too. They were difficult to feed, they took sick easily, and few veterinarians—certainly no veterinarians in Cedar Creek—knew much about them.

Jimbo lugged the cage into the pet shop and slid it into a space beside another cage, this one holding a male brown rhesus monkey. This animal jumped up and rattled the bars of his cage, hissing and spitting at the new arrival.

Rudy emerged from the rear of the store and peered at the colobus. "You got papers and all?"

"Papers? You don't need papers, Rudy. She's just what you asked for."

Rudy was taken aback. "She? What do you mean she?" He started to open the cage to take a closer look but the animal cowered in a corner, lashing out as Rudy reached in. She scratched him deeply, drawing blood.

"Dammit!" Rudy yelped in pain and pulled his hand out of the cage, sucking the blood. "I told you a male, Jimbo."

"You said 'she,'" Jimbo protested. "C'mon, man . . ."

"I said 'he.' The customer has already got a female—he wants to breed 'em. This one is no good to me at all." He shook his head and wiped the blood from his hand with a rag. The brown rhesus saw his chance, reaching into the colobus' cage and snatching the half-eaten banana, scarfing it down quickly.

"Look, man," said Jimbo. "I've got to sell her. I'll sell her cheap."

Rudy pointed to the rhesus. "I can't even sell that one. Sorry, Jimbo. I don't need to add to inventory. People who buy exotics know exactly what they want. And my guy wants a male colobus."

"Great," said Jimbo hollowly. "That's just great. What am I gonna do with her? I've got a plane to catch."

"I don't know," said Rudy, shrugging. "Maybe you could start a circus."

"Very funny."

Jimbo loaded the cage back into his car. There just wasn't time for him to take the monkey back to Biotest and make his flight. He would have to set the creature free. . . .

He drove ten or twelve miles out of town before he found a spot suitably deserted—Jimbo wasn't sure but he had a feeling that releasing a monkey into the wild was probably some kind of crime and he didn't want to be seen doing it. He dragged the cage into the woods and threw open the door. The monkey seemed reluctant to leave.

"Come on, girl. Freedom. I'd keep ya, but I'm already hitched." He kicked at the iron bars. "Look. Trees and everything. Just like home . . ." But she still refused to budge. Jimbo rattled the cage a little more and she darted out, frightened, but stopped at the edge of the underbrush, looking back at him.

Jimbo picked up a handful of gravel and threw it at her. "Git now! Go!"

The monkey scampered off, vanishing into the forest. Jimbo got back in his car and hit the highway. By the time he got to the airport he was already beginning to feel ill. . . .

The flight from California to Boston was five hours, but to Jimbo Scott it seemed endless. He wasn't feeling too good when he boarded, collapsing into his seat, glad to discover that the plane was half full and that he would get a row to himself. By the time they were midway across the continent, he was shivering, freezing cold, and clutching at the thin airline blanket for warmth. But he was also sweating, as if he were sitting in a steam room, and he had a headache so intense it felt as if his brain were caught in a vise.

"Just my luck," he murmured miserably. "Get the flu the day I start my vacation."

Jimbo could hardly bear the thought of food and he picked at the tray one of the flight attendants placed in front of him. Across the aisle, though, a four-year-old boy in full cowboy regalia noticed that Jimbo had hardly touched his dessert.

"Hey, mister . . . mister."

Jimbo opened his red-rimmed eyes. "Yeah?"

"You gonna finish that?" The little boy pointed to a cookie resting on Jimbo's tray.

"Nah," said Jimbo. "Help yourself, Sheriff."

Just as the boy reached for the cookie his grab was interrupted by his mother. "Bobby, you've had enough. Don't bother the nice man."

The kid looked beseechingly at Jimbo, asking for intervention with his eyes.

"Sorry," said Jimbo. "I don't want no trouble with the law." He closed his eyes and concentrated, as if willing the plane to go faster, hoping he could speed up time.

By the time the flight touched down in Boston, Jimbo was more sick than he had ever been before. The fever had increased in intensity, as had the headache. Now he felt a pressing fatigue and sharp pains in his joints. He was relieved to see his girlfriend Alice waiting in the throng of people standing at the arrivals gate.

"Oh, baby," he said. He almost collapsed

into her arms and held her tight while he kissed her. "Am I glad to see you."

"I missed you too," said Alice. She stepped back and looked at him. "You look like shit, baby."

"Musta ate something, or something," he said. His words were slurred and indistinct, his eyes rolling in his head. He was going to pass out.

Alice felt the panic rising. "Jimbo, honey? You okay? What's wrong?"

"Sick," said Jimbo. "Real sick. Take me home, baby. Now."

Rudy Alvarez didn't begin to feel ill until the next morning. By the time he got to his store he had the fever and chills were on him, slowing him down. By midmorning the headache had started, but he forced himself to keep working. His was a one-man operation—if he closed up shop and went home he would have lost a full day of revenue. Sick leave was a luxury he couldn't begin to afford.

He was trying to keep his mind fixed on the task at hand—feeding his tropical fish—when a customer walked in holding her Persian cat in her arms.

"Morning, Rudy," said the customer. "Lucrecia won't even touch those shredded beef wafers, so we'll have to go back to the veal . . ."

Rudy looked up, unsteady on his feet, leaning against one of the tanks for support. He wiped a handful of sweat from his flushed face.

"Are you okay, Rudy?" the woman asked, peering closely at him.

"Just fine, Mrs. Foote," he said uncertainly. "Let's get Lucrecia her veal . . ."

Wearily he pushed away from the tanks, took two or three tottering steps and then stopped. His face twitched, as if electricity were being jolted through him, and he sagged back against the fish tanks. Then he fell heavily, grabbing for the tanks, pulling them to the floor. There was an explosion of breaking glass, gushing water and flopping fish. Rudy lay sprawled in the middle of the chaos, blood beginning to ooze from his nose.

Emergency Room
Cedar Creek General Hospital

SEPTEMBER 2, 1995

The emergency room at Cedar Creek General was quiet in the mornings, the busy periods tending to be when the bars were open and schools were closed. Dr. Mascelli was in charge of the trauma team that pounced on Rudy when he was wheeled into the facility on a gurney.

The doctor immediately went for Rudy's heart, listening to the faint and irregular beat as Emma, his ER nurse, put an oxygen mask over Rudy's ashen face. Henry, a lab technician, pinched the vein in Rudy's arm and drew blood.

"C'mon, Rudy," the doctor muttered. "Help me out here. Looks like toxic shock—what's the story?"

"A friend of his said he was fine yesterday," said Emma. "This is awful sudden whatever it is."

"I've been reading about these real bad strep cases in *Newsweek*. Maybe this is one of them," said Henry.

"I guess I should subscribe," said Mascelli. "Henry, get me a blood count, chemistry profile, blood culture—the works."

Henry emptied the blood into a vacutainer. "Coming up," he said.

The lab was Henry's domain, everything arranged precisely the way Henry liked it. He loaded the blood sample into a centrifuge and turned it on, the arm spinning furiously. A few minutes of that treatment and the blood would be broken down into its component parts.

Henry settled behind his desk and turned on his radio, tuning in to the Giants' game— Henry was a big Giants fan—that was being played on the East Coast. As he listened, he toyed with the silver medic-alert bracelet he wore around his wrist.

The Giants were in a 1-to-1 tie with the Atlanta Braves. It was the eighth inning and the Giants had a man on with Matt Williams coming to bat. Gary Maddox was pitching for Atlanta, so this promised to be a classic duel—the big slugger versus the finesse pitcher.

Henry forgot the centrifuge for a moment and leaned closer to his radio. "C'mon, Matt, hammer that thing."

Williams took the first pitch as called strike, then fouled off the next two. Henry could imagine Williams digging in and staring down the pitcher, daring him to try and throw one by him.

Just then the buzzer on the centrifuge sounded. "Damn," said Henry. "Perfect timing." He lifted the lid of the machine and reached inside.

The crack of Williams' bat was distinctly audible, the radio announcer's voice filled with excitement. "It's a long ball, hit to deep right center . . . That ball is—gone!"

"Yes!" Henry pumped his fist and smashed the blood vial in his palm. The centrifuge was still spinning and it caught the blood, spraying it everywhere. Henry was drenched in blood, in his face, his eyes, his hair.

"Oh my God!" Henry rushed to the sink and doused his face with water, scrubbing the blood from his face. He had been doing bloodwork for years and Henry knew the risks involved. Blood was dirty—filthy—a polluted cocktail of viruses and microbes, never mind AIDS. . . .

Henry rinsed off and hurried down the corridor to find Dr. Mascelli. The doctor was still tending to Rudy.

"Got those cultures for me, Henry."

"Oh man," said Henry, his voice high and panicky. "I just got his blood all over me."

"Don't worry," said Mascelli calmly. "We'll draw some more and start again."

"But what about me?" said Henry. "I got his blood in my face. I could get infected with something. Something like AIDS."

"Don't worry," said Mascelli soothingly. "The chances of contagion are slight. We'll test the blood, Henry. I'm sure there's nothing to worry about."

But Henry refused to be consoled. "Maybe you should give me penicillin. I don't want to give anything to my girlfriend, you know?"

"Really? Flowers might be nice on occasion . . ." Mascelli nudged Henry in the ribs.

Henry managed to squeeze out a weak smile. "Yeah," he said. "I guess."

**Center for Disease Control
Atlanta, Georgia**

SEPTEMBER 2, 1995

Mealtimes at facilities like the CDC and USAMRIID took a little getting used to—but Robby Keough had long ago mastered the art of eating and discussing a loathsome disease at the same time.

Robby was conducting a lunchtime meeting with her two subordinates, Dr. Julio Ruiz and her primary assistant Lisa Aronson. Robby was eating a big plate of french fries and discussing the day's crop of faxes from around the country. Taken together, these daily reports composed a summary of every reported disease in the country.

"You really shouldn't eat that crap," Dr. Ruiz cautioned. "Bad for you."

Robby laughed. "Lots of ketchup, lots of salt. Here. Indulge. You're gonna love it."

But Ruiz recoiled as if she had offered him a plate of strychnine.

"Michigan," said Aronson. "We have an another outbreak of e. coli. Couple of fevers of unknown origin up in Boston. Their infectious disease docs can't seem to figure them out. They say it looks viral."

"Really? The patients wouldn't be African explorers back from some safari in Zaire, would they?"

"Well . . . No. They are a couple of American kids. They report no unusual travel."

"I'll bet you it's some atypical strain of Lyme disease and those Boston doctors missed the boat on the way to the golf course," said Ruiz.

"Lyme with petechial lesions, Julio?" said Aronson. "I don't think so . . ."

Robby froze. "What did you say?"

"I said I didn't think so," said Aronson. "No known case of Lyme has ever produced petechial lesions."

"That's because this isn't Lyme," Robby whispered. "Lisa. Get me on a plane to Boston."

7

Boston Municipal Hospital
Boston, Massachusetts

SEPTEMBER 2, 1995

Jimbo and Alice were in Boston Municipal's quarantine section, watched over by two very worried doctors. The doctors were used to dealing with disease and death, but this quick and devastating illness had unnerved them. When they heard that the Center for Disease Control had dispatched one of their most eminent virologists, they were relieved—and even more alarmed. They were delighted to hand over responsibility for the case, but frightened that a disease so deadly had chosen to manifest itself in their hospital.

Robby, along with the three doctors, entered the quarantine ward, all three of them swathed from head-to-toe in surgical scrubs and masks. She was used to the fact that doctors were almost always unflappable, determined, and calm in the face of illness and injury. These three doctors, however, were plainly scared; Robby was determined not to lose her head.

But even she found a sharp bolt of panic when she saw Jimbo Scott. A livid scarlet hemorrhagic rash painted both cheeks, and thick black blood trickled from his nose, mouth, and ears, staining the sheets.

Robby whispered to him. "James? Jimbo? Can you hear me? We're here to help you. But we need to know how you got sick. Can you talk to me? Jimbo?"

Alice was doing her best to rise from the bed. "Is he all right? Honey, are you okay?"

"Jimbo," said Robby urgently. "Have you been in contact with any animals?"

For a moment, it looked as if Jimbo were trying to summon up the strength to say something, but the effort proved too much. His eyes went blank and life slipped out of him.

Robby sighed and stood up, then gathered the doctors in a corner of the room for a hurried, whispered conference. "Did he tell you anything?" Robby asked. "Did he give you any idea how he may have gotten it?"

The doctors looked glum. "No. He had no idea where he got it or how. It hit him yesterday."

"And killed him today," said one. "What in God's name is this thing?"

"I'm here to find out," said Robby briskly. She had successfully managed to hide her own feelings of anxiety over this disease. "We'll need a postmortem."

"No way," said one of the men. "I'm not going to slip and cut myself and get whatever the fuck he had."

Robby turned away in disgust. "How about you?" she asked the older man.

He shuffled his feet and tried not to meet her gaze. "Uh . . . I don't do autopsies . . ."

Robby turned to the third. "I guess it's you then."

The doctor nodded glumly. "I guess it is . . ."

Alice was still trying to rise from the bed. "He's dead!" she wailed hysterically. She tried to snatch at Robby's scrubs. "Don't let him die, please. Oh, Jimbo . . ."

Robby knelt by her side. "Alice," she said soothingly, "we're taking care of him. But we need to know how he got sick. Did he tell you anything? Anything at all?"

But the woman was too frantic and too sick to answer any questions now. Alice lay back on the pillows, moaning pathetically.

"One of you guys stay with her," Robby ordered. "Try to calm her down. Talk to her. Record anything she tells you—anything, understand?"

Like chastened schoolboys, the two doctors nodded. Robby turned to the third doctor. "And you're coming with me, right?"

"Right."

"What's your name?"

"Hampton."

"Okay, Dr. Hampton, let's get to it."

It took fifteen minutes to get a plastic pathology lab tent erected around a table in the hospital's autopsy room and then orderlies wheeled Jimbo Scott's body into the enclosure, trundling him along gingerly, as if they were transporting a shipment of nitroglycerine. Scott was naked, his entire body marbled with horrible, brownish lesions. He looked as if he had been flogged to death, each lesion a bloody lash mark, his face gaunt and wasted, as if the disease had eaten away the body from within. Robby and Hampton, both dressed now in Racal biosafety suits, stood over the cadaver, sickened by the ravages that had been visited on Jimbo Scott.

"I . . . I've never seen anything like this," said Hampton. Doctors had notoriously strong stomachs, but Robby could see that Hampton was rattled, repulsed by the sight before him.

"Calm down, Doctor," said Robby. "You've been dissecting cadavers since your first year in medical school. Just go slow. Maximum sharps precautions."

Hampton licked his lips and exhaled heavily. Sweat dripped from his forehead, fogging his visor. He took a scalpel from the tray at his side and held the blade above the mottled skin of Jimbo Scott's sternum. His hand was trembling and he fought to control it, desperate to collect himself.

"Okay," said Robby. She could see that

Hampton was trying, but he would be of little use in this procedure. "Give me the scalpel. You assist."

Hampton's shoulders slumped, as if he had suddenly had a huge burden lifted from his back. "Right." He turned the blade, carefully giving her the scalpel handle first. With only a split section of hesitation she lowered the knife onto Scott's skin and made her first incision, cutting him from the chest to the pubic bone. Sluggish brown blood welled up around the incision and trickled onto the stainless-steel table and collected in the drain beneath.

Once Robby had cracked the chest, cutting through tough muscle surrounding the rib cage and through the lattice of bone, the extent of the havoc wreaked by this disease became apparent. Hampton gazed into the thoracic cavity as if looking into a pit of horror.

"Heaven help us all," he whispered.

Robby and Hampton emerged from the autopsy exhausted and shaken. Hampton immediately went to the doctors' lounge to lie down and to try to forget what he had witnessed. Robby, however, was still on the job. The first thing she did was call Sam, reaching him at home.

"We know now that he worked at an animal quarantine facility in San Jose, California." Robby didn't even bother to say hello, as if any pleasantries would be nothing more than a distraction. "He might have gotten it there. We're monitoring all his coworkers there."

"The host might be there," said Sam. "Don't let a single animal out of there."

"We'll quarantine the whole place," said Robby. "I've already quarantined the Boston Med staff, the EMS crew, all the girl's neighbors . . . People are scared here, Sam. I had to force one of the doctors to assist in the post."

"What did you find?" The animals in the USAMRIID lab had all undergone autopsies, but this was the first time anyone had seen the effects of Motaba on human tissue.

"What did I find? Sam, when I opened this guy up . . . It was like a bomb had gone off inside him. Liver, pancreas, kidneys, spleen—all the organs had liquefied. The basic structure was just *gone* . . ." Robby sighed heavily. "You were right, Sam. I should have forced the alert."

Sam knew she was feeling guilty, as if the deaths were her fault, and he rushed to reassure her. "Robby, that alert wouldn't have helped us with these two kids. Get tissue samples to the CDC. Confirm that it is Motaba. Anybody else showing symptoms up there?"

"No. Not yet. The CDC is sending out a Stage Three Alert . . . Any new cases and we'll be hearing about them in a hurry, I guess." The uncertainty and fear in her voice were obvious.

"How about you?" Sam asked softly. "You okay, Rob?"

"Yes," she said. "I'm tired, that's all . . . This is what we do, Sam."

"What about the girl?"

"Alice?" said Robby. "She died while I was in post. But she wasn't on the plane."

"So she met him at the airport?"

"The plane got in at nine o'clock. She was admitted to the hospital at six this morning."

"So, at most, we're talking about a twenty-four-hour incubation period, right?"

Robby groaned. "I can't believe it . . . Shit, Sam, this thing moves so fast."

"Yes it does!" In contrast to Robby, Sam Daniels sounded up, almost encouraged. "So if nobody gets sick within twenty-four hours, we're in the clear, right?"

Robby was silent for a moment. "This just isn't like you, Sam, you know that?"

"What? What isn't like me?"

"This imagining best-case scenarios."

"How can you say that when I still believe that there's hope for us? It's nice being back in the game with you, kid. I'll stand watch. You get some sleep."

"Right," she said with a hollow laugh. "With my eyes wide open."

"Keep your legs crossed."

The monkey had wandered deep into the forest, scuttling through the shadows, running from tree to tree, hiding from the dangers she was sure lurked in this alien place. Huge, threatening redwoods towered over her, filling the night sky with massive, menacing silhouettes.

The creature was hungry, but she could find none of the fruits and nuts that she lived on in her native place. Tentatively, she reached for a pine cone and gnawed on it. But it was not food.

Alone and hungry, the monkey cried fearfully and then ran further into the night.

8

Starlight Theater
Cedar Creek, California

SEPTEMBER 2, 1995

The movie was a hit, a comedy—it had just opened in Cedar Creek and there was a big crowd for the seven o'clock showing. Waiting in line were the medical technician from the hospital, Henry, and his girlfriend Corrine. Henry was feeling feverish and sweaty and a cough was starting to come on, but he had insisted on going out. He figured that a movie might take his mind off his incipient illness and make him forget the nagging unease he felt at the back of his mind. He said nothing to Corrine about the incident at work earlier that day—why worry her unnecessarily? If he was really getting sick then this was probably nothing more life-threatening than a case of the flu. One thing Henry did know for sure—it wasn't AIDS. You couldn't get AIDS in a day. He let that little nugget of information reassure him.

Still, he felt lousy . . . So lousy, he couldn't concentrate on the movie. Corrine and all the people around him seemed to be enjoying themselves, erupting into laughter every few minutes. Henry wiped the sweat from his brow and coughed violently, the noise of his cough covered by a loud and lengthy burst of laughter from the audience. A tiny droplet of saliva, microscopically small, shot from his mouth and sailed through the air, riding the warm currents of air in the packed room like a bird over the desert.

The bead of moisture almost alit on a box of popcorn sitting in the lap of a little girl, but a gust of air lifted it again and carried it across the auditorium and landed it in the open mouth of a man who was laughing up-roariously.

Henry continued to cough, spewing dozens more drops into the darkness. Corrine leaned forward and patted him on the back. She was worried—her boyfriend sounded terrible.

"You okay, Henry?"

"Yeah, yeah," he said, wiping his eyes. "Just thirsty. I need some water."

"I'll get it," she said, half rising from her seat.

"No, no, it's okay. I could use the air . . ." He struggled out of the seat and stumbled along the row and up the aisle.

The show in the second theater in the complex had not started yet, so the lobby was crowded. Henry felt his tongue dry and rough in his mouth and his throat felt terribly parched. The headache was beginning and he was unaware that his eyes were beginning to turn blood red. He swayed toward the concession stand, the girl behind the counter and a black woman customer looked at him warily. The woman held a toddler by the hand. The look on his face suggested that he was insane, his red eyes were frightening.

"Help me . . ." he mumbled. His voice was almost a croak his mouth was so dry. Then he doubled over in another spasm of coughing.

"You'll have to wait your turn," said the salesgirl. She wore a name tag that identified her as TRACY.

Coughing, Henry lunged for the edge of the glass display case. "Please," he managed to gasp. *"Help me."* Then his strength ran out and he fell, sliding down the counter and sprawling on the floor.

Intensive Care Unit
Cedar Creek Hospital

SEPTEMBER 2, 1995

When Henry regained consciousness, his head ached horribly and he felt the sharp pains in his joints. His fever had not abated. Dr. Mascelli was standing over him, looking down with pity in his eyes.

"Henry—we caught it early. And you're

going to make it." The doctor spoke with a conviction he did not feel. "But I need you to fight."

Henry stared at him with blank eyes, as if not quite able to grasp the meaning of the doctor's words.

The public address speaker crackled. "Dr. Mascelli to ER stat. Dr. Mascelli to ER stat." "Stat" was hospital jargon for "immediately."

"Look who's here . . ." said Mascelli.

Henry's eyes shifted to his girlfriend. Corrine took his hand and squeezed it tight. "Hi . . . You gotta fight, okay?" she said. "You gotta fight it." Then she started to cough. . . .

Mascelli rushed out and dashed down the corridor to the emergency room. Two paramedics were wheeling in a girl, the sheet half covering her, but the doctor could see that she was wearing a uniform and a name tag—TRACY. Her father was running alongside, holding her hand.

"Doctor—she got sick so fast. She got home from work and said she didn't feel well. I thought it was flu, but she fainted in the bathroom. She's burning up . . . Doc . . . She's burning up."

"I'm sure she'll be all right," said Mascelli. "Let's get her admitted and I'll be right with you." The doctor raced down the hallway to his office and took down a book from his medical library. It was a dictionary of infectious diseases, arranged by symptoms. Mascelli thumbed through the pages frantically, reading a few lines and then skipping to the next. He knew it was futile, but he had to try. The problem was that so many viruses began with fever, headache, and other flulike symptoms. What set this new disease apart from the others was the amazing speed of contagion and infection—and there was nothing in his virology text that even came close.

He closed the book with a loud snap. "Damn!"

Emma, the emergency room nurse knocked on his office door and leaned into the room. "Doctor, we have a problem . . . I think you better come take a look."

The emergency room was full of people, all of them from the movie theater. There were the people who had sat in the same row as Henry, unwitting recipients of the moisture he had coughed into the closed atmosphere of the theater, the black woman from the candy counter was there too, as was the little girl she had been holding in her arms.

"Oh my God," said Mascelli. "What is going on here? They can't *all* be sick."

"They keep coming in," said Emma. "What's wrong with these people?"

Mascelli shook his head. "I don't know, Emma. *I don't know.*" But he knew what he had to do. "Emma, get me the County Health Department. Now."

The little girl was coughing uncontrollably, her mother holding her tight. "My baby!" she wailed. "Please, somebody help me!"

Mascelli surveyed the chaos and confusion in his normally placid emergency room. He scarcely noticed that his fax machine had buzzed and clicked on. The piece of paper scrolling out of the unit was headed: "Center for Disease Control, Atlanta, Emergency Bulletin . . ."

Center for Disease Control
War Room, Atlanta

SEPTEMBER 3, 1995

A large but crowded space, the war room was the nerve center of the Center for Disease Control. Doctors and staff manned banks of phones and fax machines, all of them talking on the phone while staring at a large electronic map of the United States which dominated the room. A red circle blinked on Boston and the time there was slotted up on a digital clock. It was 2:43 A.M., and the last minutes of the incubation period were fast ticking away.

As leader of the team working on the Motaba outbreak, Robby sat at the large desk in the middle of the room. She too was working the phones.

"Are you sure?" she said. "Every last one? Great! That's really great. Thank you, Doctor." She hung up and turned to Reynolds, Aronson, and Ruiz. They had been waiting anxiously throughout the conversation.

Robby was beaming. "The airline passengers checked out clean," she said. Her happiness overwhelmed her exhaustion. "No further infection at Boston General, either."

Ruiz clapped his hands. "And no reports from any other Boston hospital. We are in the clear, people."

Reynolds leaned forward and pressed a button on the console. As the red ring circling Boston clicked off, a cheer rose from the workers in the war room. All were exhausted and relieved, but with the crisis at an end, they were lighthearted and giddy, elated that something so deadly had been contained and with so few fatalities.

It was Lisa Aronson who noticed the lone fax coming out of the machine. She ripped it from the roll of paper and read it. Her euphoria vanished, her smiled faded, and grim-faced, she handed it to Robby Keough.

She read the fax and then looked to Reynolds. "Trouble," she said.

The room was hushed now and all eyes were focused on Keough. She leaned down and pressed another button. A red light came on, this one just north of San Francisco. Robby Keough closed her eyes. "Fifteen cases. Oh my God . . ."

General Ford opened the front door of his house, dressed in his pajamas and robe. Sam Daniels was dressed in his battle dress fatigues. Both men looked stunned.

"Sorry to bother you so late at night, General."

"Come in, Sam." He led Sam through the house and into his study. The general sank down behind his desk.

"Another outbreak? Besides the one in Boston? Are you sure?"

"We're sure." Daniels leaned forward. "Sir, I know you're reluctant, but we're the only two agencies capable of dealing with the virus. That's why I want to get out of here tonight. They need all the help they can get."

Ford looked at him a moment, almost as if he didn't recognize him. When he did finally speak, his voice was low and hollow. "Sorry, Sam. Can't do it."

"Why? Why in God's name would you keep me out of there? It makes no sense!"

"It's a civilian matter now," said Ford. But his voice carried little conviction. "The CDC is on it. Let them do their job. Besides, we don't have the charter."

Sam Daniels was no stickler for the rules and procedure at the best of times. Faced with an outbreak of the deadliest disease he had ever encountered in his long career, the regulations faded to insignificance. "Fuck the charter! Billy, you're a doctor. We've been colleagues in the lab. We've been friends for twenty years."

There was a little more steel in Ford's voice now. "Yes, we're friends. But I'm also your boss. I run this outfit. It's not run by committee. You do what I say you do. I'm your boss. I have my boss. Is that clear to you?"

"Yeah?" said Sam bitterly. "Why don't you get your boss on the phone? Tell McClintock to get me on a plane before you both commit mass murder."

That struck too close to the nerve. Ford was angry now, recovering strength and resolve. He stood and faced Sam down. "Colonel, I'm gonna suggest you shut up now before you say something else you're going to be sorry for. Remember who you're talking to."

"Who am I talking to?" Sam demanded. Having his team yanked off Motaba, followed by this kind of obdurate reluctance to do the smart thing could only mean that there was more at work here than a mere desire to maintain the army charter.

"Sam . . ." the general cautioned.

Sam paced the room. "No, really. Who am I talking to? I don't know. I don't know if I'm talking to USAMRIID, McClintock, Dugway, the fucking CIA." He stared hard at Billy Ford, as if trying to read his thoughts. "Will you tell me who I'm talking to?"

"This conversation is over," said Ford curtly, but he avoided Daniels' gaze.

"Can you? Tell me who I'm talking to."

There was a long moment of silence. Ford seemed to be struggling with himself and for an instant it seemed that he would break down and say what was really on his mind. But then the soldier in his soul reasserted itself.

"You will be on the plane for New Mexico

this morning. I suggest you go home and pack or do whatever it is you have to do—And do it now, Colonel."

Sam called Robby from his car as he drove over the back roads of rural Maryland at high speed. He was angry and his driving reflected the intensity of his ire. He took the corners too fast and on any piece of straight road he pushed the gas pedal to the floor, screaming along the highway.

"Robby, don't go near this thing again."

"I'm leaving with a team in an hour," she said firmly.

"You don't have to go! Just coordinate everything from CDC. Send your best people."

"No. I'm going. If this is the real thing, I need to be there. You were in Zaire. You know what I'm talking about."

Her words were determined but she sounded so tired Sam half expected her to doze off on the phone. Furthermore, much as he wanted to go to the disease site himself, he hated the idea of Robby going. For once, it wasn't professional jealousy, it was fear. He didn't want her anywhere near Motaba—she had taken too many risks already.

"Robby—"

"You'd be in Cedar Creek right now if Ford would let you go. Right?"

"He should," said Sam. "He knows better."

" 'Course he does. There's your Army for you. Sam . . ."

Sam sounded really desperate now. "All I'm saying is you don't have to suit up. You don't have to put yourself at risk. For all I know this thing flies through rubber gloves. It's a stone hard killer!"

Robby smiled. "Thanks for trying to talk me out of it."

Sam could tell that he was never going to change her mind. "Fine," he said, resigned. "Do whatever you have to do." He hung up and thought for a moment. He too had a plan.

Dover Air Force Base
Dover, Maryland

SEPTEMBER 3, 1995, 4:32 A.M.

It was well before dawn, but AFB Dover was bustling as usual—no matter the hour, this base never closed down completely. One of the C-130 transport planes assigned to the USAMRIID flight was packed and waiting when Sam Daniels got out to Dover, the pilot just finishing his preflight check. Daniels took a quick look at the flight plan and saw that there had been no change of heart on the part of General Ford. The filed flight plan was for Dover, Maryland to Albuquerque, New Mexico.

"Dammit," Daniels whispered. He slipped out of the plane and crossed the tarmac, walking straight into the operations building. There was a young noncom on duty that morning, Sergeant Wolfe, who jumped to his feet and saluted—he was not expecting a full colonel to pay him a visit at quite so early an hour. And Wolfe couldn't help but notice that this colonel did not look happy. It was not an auspicious start to the day.

Daniels scowled at Wolfe for a moment. "All right . . . who fucked up, Sergeant? Why hasn't my pilot been informed of the new orders?"

"New orders—?" Behind Wolfe, on the wall of the room, was a chart listing all of the scheduled flights in and out of Dover for that day. Daniels and the USAMRIID team was right there where they were supposed to be: 0500 for Albuquerque, New Mexico. "Sir, I'm not quite sure that I—"

"General Ford called me at 0200, told me to get my ass to Cedar Creek. You didn't get the dispatch?"

Wolfe shook his head vigorously. "No, sir. We have you leaving for Albuquerque in twenty minutes as scheduled, sir."

Daniels groaned. "I'm not going to fucking Albuquerque, I'm going to Cedar Creek, California! I'm in a hurry! This is an emergency. Please get General Ford on the phone for confirmation. Now! Sergeant!"

The young man picked up the phone with great reluctance. In the military realm it was unusual—not to say dangerous—for a lowly tech sergeant to pick up the phone and call a brigadier general. However, getting all the proper clearances was the first order of business—he had to make the call.

It was Sam who thought the better of it. He stopped and grabbed the phone from the sergeant's hand. "No. Don't get a confirmation."

"I'll call, sir," Wolfe insisted.

"No! Are you crazy! Wake him up at 2:30! In the morning? Redirect us on my authority. Call the tower and tell them to change my flight plan. Do it! Put your finger on the phone."

"Redirect on your authority, sir?" the sergeant asked nervously. "But this could mean my stripes, sir."

"Put your finger on the phone!"

If Sergeant Wolfe had summoned up all his courage and actually called General Ford, he would not have found that Colonel Daniels was lying. Ford was not in bed, he wasn't even at home.

After Daniels left earlier that evening, Ford had gotten dressed, quickly putting on his uniform, then drove to USAMRIID. He made his way to a storage facility in the subterranean sections of the main building, walking along a lengthy row of tall stainless steel doors. He stopped in front of one and punched a number into the keypad of the combination lock. A cloud of vapor escaped as the air lock seal broke and the massive door swung open. Within the refrigerated compartment were stacks of stout plastic bags, orange-brown antiserum bags, each one stenciled with the designation number E-1101.

The general stared at them for a moment and then began removing the bags. This antiserum had been undisturbed in this storage chamber for almost thirty years, a secret store of a substance that, officially, did not exist. Ford had created the drug with his own hands—never imagining that there would come a day when it would be needed, right here on home ground.

9

**Dugway Proving Ground
Western Utah**

SEPTEMBER 3, 1995, 5:09 A.M.

The United States Army owned vast tracts of the Great Salt Desert in Utah, hundreds of square miles of rocky, barren land, strictly off limits to the public. There were three interlocking facilities: the Wendover Range, the Desert Test Center, and Dugway Proving Grounds, some of the most secure real estate on the North American continent. In the sparse civilian settlements on the edge of these bases all kinds of dark rumors circulated as to the activities within. The stories usually centered on UFO's and ultra-secret aircraft—no one ever hinted at the possibility that Dugway was the center for American germ and virological warfare. In addition, Dugway was the private kingdom of Major General Donald McClintock.

The general was hunkered down in one of the huge concrete bunkers, sitting in the middle of the Dugway Command Center situation room, watching the computer-generated image of northern California on the enormous video screen. The map centered on Cedar Creek.

McClintock scarcely glanced at it as he spoke on the phone. He had General Ford on the line and was rapping out orders.

"The governor of California has asked the President for federal assistance. You will proceed there and assume medical command of the First Battalion of the Eighth Infantry."

"Yes, sir."

"This is a full flash alert. I want transmission rates for all insect, animal, marine, and human vectors. If this thing is spreading, I want to know how fast and where . . . meanwhile we are in a go mode for Clean Sweep." McClintock was in his element. The only thing he liked better than an involved, covert operation, was the delicious feeling of command.

Ford was less thrilled. Operation Clean Sweep was as drastic a plan that existed in the army playbook—he couldn't allow it to unfold here and now. The general eyed the sack of E-1101 lying on his desk in front of him.

"Mac," he said, "you and I both know we could throw these people a lifeline."

McClintock almost laughed at the idea. "Negative, General. Proceed with conventional containment. Maintain an absolute media blackout and make sure you keep your subordinates in line. You know who I'm talking about."

"Yes, sir," said Ford. He stared hard at the bag of serum.

"Good. Anything else?"

"No, sir."

As the C-130 taxied into position, Sam Daniels strapped himself into his seat and examined a high detailed map of western and central California. He appeared to be untroubled that he was in the process of committing a court-martial offense—more than one: dereliction of duty, failure to perform, desertion, insubordination—any one of those charges could earn him a stiff term in the stockade at Leavenworth. It was something he would have to worry about later—right now, Motaba was the enemy.

Casey Schuler seemed equally unconcerned. Salt, on the other hand, was troubled, acutely aware that all he had worked for, had striven for was about to go down the tubes. He glanced out of the small window, watching the lights of the terminal grow smaller. There was still time to protest, to get off the plane and save himself and his career. . . .

But somehow he couldn't bring himself to do it. He had been accepted as a member of this team. To leave now would be to commit an act of betrayal that he was sure he couldn't stomach.

Casey could see Salt's distress. "Listen,

Major," he said, "you understand that Colonel Daniels is not *actually* bucking authority—right, Sam?" He smiled reassuringly. "See, he's just doing what he does best, which is to anticipate orders. Come with us! Risk your career. Maybe even end up in Leavenworth. Right, Sam?"

Sam Daniels looked away from the map for a moment. "Goes for you too, Case."

"I got a note from my mom."

Sam smiled at Salt. "You are under no military obligation to come with us, Salt. But if you do, I will take full responsibility."

"Which only means that they hang him first."

The engines were hitting peak revs now and turning toward the head of the runway. Salt hesitated before speaking.

"Sirs," he said slowly, "my career is in the military. I have a wife. I have a kid." He shrugged and smiled weakly.

Sam nodded. "We understand . . ."

"Open the hatch!" Casey yelled.

Then Salt stopped. "On the other hand, if this thing is as bad as we say it is, Leavenworth will be the least of my worries."

"Is that a yes?" Casey asked.

"I think so."

"Close the hatch!"

Cedar Creek State Park
Cedar Creek California

SEPTEMBER 3, 1995, 5:45 A.M.

By chance the monkey had come upon a campground, a collection of vacationers' tents pitched in the small, pretty national park on the outskirts of the little town. Under the cover of darkness she had scurried from tent to tent scavenging, desperate for something to eat. She had found some bits and pieces, some edible garbage stuffed into cans, the remains of last night's barbecue, half-eaten apples, and some bread that campers had scattered around to attract birds.

She gathered up her treasure trove of food, retreating to a dark corner to eat. But as soon as she had settled, she cocked an ear, listening to a sound the likes of which she had never heard before. It was a deep, bass rumble, so low-pitched that the air seemed to vibrate, a sound so resonant it could be felt more than heard.

Suddenly, the sky was alive with noise and light as a squadron of helicopters roared overhead, descending on the still-sleeping town. The choppers touched down at a dozen predetermined points, soldiers pouring out of the machines, cutting off roads and bridges isolating Cedar Creek from the outside world. . . .

By dawn, two perimeters had been established, inner and outer security rings completely encircling the town. Per orders, no one was allowed out and the only personnel permitted entry was the column of trucks from the CDC.

The second wave of invaders arrived in full daylight, a flight of heavy transport helicopters, mammoth Sikorsky CH-54 Tarhe sky cranes carrying prefabricated portions of a BL-4 lab. They hovered over the parking lot of the hospital maneuvering the sections of the building into place. The noise from the huge, powerful engines was deafening and made the ground tremble underfoot.

The entire town was awake now, flooding the streets, a panic-stricken crowd demanding to know what was going on. The largest group converged on the hospital, where they were met by local and state policemen who were drawn up behind barricades. Every cop was wearing a gas mask and held a shotgun in gloved hands.

Robby, Aronson, and Ruiz, dressed in full Racal biosafety suits watched, but the already angry crowd seemed to become even more upset when they caught sight of these people dressed for the most extreme danger.

An angry man—the father of the theater employee Tracy—elbowed his way to the head of the crowd and pushed up against one of the cops.

"Nobody's tellin' us what's goin' on!"

"Simmer down," said the policeman. "Just simmer down." But behind the mask and the riot gear, the cop was nothing more than a kid, too scared to do much more than stand there and hope for the best. There were tears in the young man's eyes.

The three CDC doctors were met inside the hospital by the two most important officials of the little town of Cedar Creek.

A beefy white-haired man stepped forward. "I'm Ray Fowler, chief of police. This is Mayor Gaddis."

"Roberta Keough, from the Center for Disease Control," said Robby. "My colleagues, Drs. Aronson and Ruiz."

The mayor looked at them with worried eyes. "Cedar Creek is a small town, Doctor. We're like family. Everybody is scared and we don't know what to tell them—"

"We're here to help you with that," said Robby. "I'll be in charge."

"You?" Mayor Gaddis looked bewildered. "I thought *he* was in charge." The man pointed toward the emergency room receiving bay. Sam Daniels was standing over a newly admitted patient, trying to examine her, but precise movements were all but impossible, because he too was wearing a Racal biosafety suit. Robby gaped for a moment, then walked over to him.

"Sam," she said, "what are you doing here?"

"Hi, Robby. We've just set up the mobile BL-4."

"But what are you *doing* here? I thought that Ford sent you to New Mexico," she said, still amazed to find him here. Amazed but pleased. For all his unorthodoxy and his headstrong manner, there was no one better qualified to be working on this disease site.

"He did," said Sam shortly. There was really nothing else to be said on the subject. She knew instantly that Sam had disobeyed an order from a superior. That he would do something like that was so obvious to anyone who knew him, Robby was surprised that it had never occurred to Ford; perhaps it had.

"We've isolated patients in C Wing," said Sam, leading her through the hospital. "Robby . . . don't hurt yourself."

The makeshift isolation ward was crammed with beds. The two biosuited doctors walked down the rows, the sounds of their own breathing loud in their ears. They passed bed after bed of Motaba patients, in some the disease was more advanced than others. But all were rushing toward death at a terrifying rate of speed.

"Apparently they were all infected at a movie theater," said Sam. "That was just yesterday . . ."

Robby shook her head. "So many . . ."

Nurses dressed in respirators were packing Tracy in ice, piling up steaming plastic bags around her shriveled body. She was out of her mind, delirious with a high fever, her skin was so hot the ice seemed to melt on contact.

Casey and Salt were there too, going from bed to bed, attempting to interview the patients who hadn't already declined into delirium or coma. The details were always the same—they went to the movies, they went home or out to eat and became ill. There was nothing out of the ordinary, nothing to suggest that this was anything more than random infection.

Robby looked from patient to patient and felt helpless, devastated. The exhaustion and despair of the last few days seemed to overwhelm her.

"That guy over there—Henry Seward,"

said Casey. "He probably brought it into the theater. His girlfriend said that he was feverish and had a cough, a bad cough."

Robby and Sam exchanged a glance. They were both thinking the same thing—something was wrong, something didn't add up in Seward's case.

"So many, so fast . . ." Robby was thinking hard. "This didn't happen on the plane. What's happening here."

"Which one is Henry?" Sam asked.

Casey pointed. Sam walked over and looked down at Henry. He was terribly ill, gasping for breath, his eyes blood red and unseeing. Gently, Sam raised Henry's wrist and saw that he was wearing a medic-alert bracelet. Stamped into the silver metal was the word "asthmatic."

Dr. Mascelli rushed into the room and tapped Sam on the shoulder. "Dr. Daniels, come with me. There's something I think you should see."

Mascelli walked Sam briskly out of the isolation ward and down the corridor.

"The patients in the orthopedics ward," said Mascelli breathlessly. "They were already here when this disease started showing up. None of them have had contact with any of the patients in isolation . . ."

The four orthopedic patients lay on their beds, all of them wearing casts, a couple of them were in traction. Mascelli pointed to the patient nearest the door. He had a lesion on his skin, a cough and a rising fever.

"First stage Motaba," Sam whispered. He looked around the room and saw an air conditioning vent set high up in the wall of the room. Daniels could imagine the whole thing, the ventilation system that lay inside the walls, the vents and the ducts, the conduits that held the whole setup together. The air passing from ward to ward. . . .

Behind his Plexiglas shield, Sam Daniels paled. "It's airborne," he said.

10

The helicopter carrying General Ford into the disease sector touched down at the landing zone at 8 A.M. He was out of his seat before the pilot killed the engine, striding toward the temporary command center, a well fortified and defended prefab blockhouse set on a hill commanding the town. An escort of four MP's scurried out behind him, taking up positions around Ford as if they were bodyguards.

Waiting for him at the edge of the LZ was the acting commander of the operation, Lieutenant Colonel Briggs. He was a solid-looking, gray-haired man, but he seemed slight in stature compared to Ford.

"General Ford, sir." The colonel saluted smartly. "I am Lieutenant Colonel Briggs. Welcome."

"Thank you, Colonel. Sit rep?"

Briggs took up his position at the general's elbow. "Well sir, by 0620 hours this morning we've had an inner and outer perimeter established. Since that time, no one has violated our cordon. Prior to that I can't give you any guarantees."

Ford nodded. "Two thousand six hundred and eighteen people live in this town." He glanced at his watch. "I want every one of them accounted for by nine this morning. Guarantee me that, Briggs."

"Very well, sir. We're on it."

"Good." Ford walked into the command center, giving it a cursory inspection. There was a team of signal corpsmen at the few

desks, busy establishing contact with the outside world. Bulletin boards and video monitors lined the walls and the whole room
hummed with quiet, efficient industry. As the
men looked up they recognized the general
stars on Ford's epaulets and they jumped to
their feet, saluting smartly.

"We've put you in here, sir," said Briggs.
There was a door stenciled COMMANDER and
an office beyond. It was furnished with an
army issue gun metal gray desk, a hard chair,
and a gleaming, sophisticated communications console set against one wall.

"By the way, Briggs," said Ford, as if it
were only an afterthought, "Colonel Sam
Daniels, USAMRIID, is in town, against orders. Locate him. Arrest him. Understand?"

"Yes, sir." Unlike Daniels, it would never
occur to Briggs to disobey an order.

Robby and Sam rushed out of the hospital
and ran smack straight into the angry crowd.
It had grown in size and the panic level
had been pushed to the breaking point. The
instant they saw the doctors, protected be-

hind their futuristic space suits, the crowd turned into a mob, shoving and screaming, desperate for some information.

"Are you in charge?" shrieked a wild-eyed woman. "Please! Tell us what's going on."

"Yeah! What the hell is going on here."

An elderly man wearing an American Legion cap, Cedar Creek Post, jammed right up against Sam. "You can't keep us here—we have rights!"

A young woman, a wailing infant in her arms, looked to Robby as if she might get some pity from a woman. "What's happening to us?" she asked, sobbing. "Tell me what's going on. You can't do this to us!"

It was a struggle, but Robby and Sam did manage to shove their way through the crowd. They kept their faces blank, trying to keep emotion from their features.

Within the BL-4 lab they found Salt sitting at a bench, peering into the barrel of a microscope. He looked up as they entered. "It's mutated," he said.

That was no surprise. "Show us," Daniels ordered.

Salt hit a switch, turning on the large video monitor built into one wall. He relayed the images from his microscope onto the screen. The monitor was split. On the left was the familiar strain of Motaba, the specimen magnified a million times. On the right was the mutated strain.

"The sample on the left is from Jimbo Scott," said Salt, pointing out the sharp edges of the principal sample. "That's the same as the one we brought back from Zaire. Pure African strain. We might not know where he got it, but we know who he got it from—the host."

"Wherever *it* may be," muttered Casey.

"On the right is the sample from Henry Seward," Salt continued. "Call it the Cedar Creek strain." He walked up to the screen and ran his gloved fingers over the contours of the image. "See this roughness here, the dimpling—"

Casey got it immediately. "I'm getting different serological responses. Wild guess—the protein coat has changed," he said. "It allows it to survive in the air."

"So now it spreads like flu," said Sam. "Like the measles. All right, Casey, tree of death?"

There was white board on the wall next to the video monitor, rough circles scrawled there. Each circle contained a name of an infected patient and each was linked with arrows leading to other circles. The schematic was incomplete. Casey picked up the magic marker and started to fill in the blanks.

"Assuming that the new strain originates with Henry Seward," he said. "Bing bang bong—Henry infects the theater."

"Back, back," urged Sam. "You have to go further back than that, Casey."

"Okay . . . Henry Seward is a lab technician, does a lot of blood work, but Mascelli says he was careful, meticulous. Until yesterday. Yesterday, Henry has a mishap. He is accidentally sprayed with blood in a centrifuge. A sample taken from one Rudy Alvarez . . ."

"And what do we know about him?" asked Sam. "Tell me about Alvarez."

"Zip. Dead before we got here," said Casey. "But listen—Alvarez died from the original strain. Seward died from the new strain. But they're too close in the tree for the virus to have spontaneously mutated . . . So I think the host animal is carrying both strains."

"Alvarez and Scott," said Sam. "What's the connection?"

"I'm looking for one but I can't find it," said Casey apologetically.

Robby was flipping through Rudy's chart, scanning the details quickly.

Robby held up the chart. "*Alvarez owned a pet store.* Right here—" She stabbed the page with a finger. "It says that Alvarez owned a pet store, right here in Cedar Creek."

Sam Daniels was flabbergasted. "I'm learning this now? He got it from one of his animals. The host is *there.* Tell me I'm not the first one to figure this out." He looked from one face to another. "Somebody. Tell me."

"We just got this information, Sam."

"If the host is there and Casey's right, it's carrying the antibodies for both strains."

"I'm at the pet store," said Robby.

"Salt, you start on the new strain from scratch. Casey—blood test."

Then Sam was off and running.

There was only one way to make sure that the virus stayed put and that was to cooperate fully with the military—Sam knew he had no other choice. He was putting his own skin in jeopardy, he knew that too, but the greater consequences were so much more devastating that he had to risk it. He had no alternative.

Sam commandeered a Hummer from the guarded motor pool behind the hospital and gunned it out of the lot. Between the hospital and the inner perimeter checkpoint, however, his vehicle was set upon by more angry inhabitants. They closed around his jeep, pounding on the metal panels, their voices fused into a single confused bellow, a mixture of cries of rage and naked wails of terror.

A squad of heavily armed soldiers, every man draped in bizarre-looking chemical warfare suits charged the crowd, shoving them back just long enough to clear a path for the Hummer. Sam hit the gas hard and drove through the open gate and into the command center compound.

Ford was sitting at his desk reading faxes

and radio traffic from his superiors in the outside world. The ever-attendant Briggs at his side reached for the Beretta clipped to his belt when Sam came bursting into the room.

Ford hardly flinched. He looked up calmly and smiled at Daniels, as if he were expecting him to drop in. "Sam. There you are. Colonel Briggs has been looking for you." He turned to Briggs, smiling affably. "Colonel, please place this man under arrest."

"Yes, sir."

Sam raised his hands, as if to push Briggs away. "Wait. We're in deep shit. The virus has mutated, Billy. It's aerosolized."

Ford grimaced. "Colonel Briggs, would you excuse us?" When Briggs had gone, Ford turned on Daniels. "What are you talking about? Motaba is only spread by direct human contact. You told me so yourself."

"I know that's what I said. But now I'm telling you we're facing a new strain here." Sam's voice was flat and matter-of-fact. "It spreads like flu."

"That's impossible."

"It has happened, General. Go to the hospital. Go and see for yourself. Better yet, go without a mask—you'll see much more clearly that way."

"Oh, Jesus . . ." said Ford softly. It really did sound as if he were praying.

"We've got nineteen dead already," said Sam. His voice was low and intense. "There are hundreds more infected. It's spreading like a brushfire. We gotta isolate the sick, I mean *really* isolate 'em, we gotta get everybody else into their houses and keep them there."

"We're doing it, Sam."

"No! You're not! I know because I just drove through a hundred people and if one of them has it, ten of them have it now; one of them gets out of Cedar Creek and we've got a big fucking problem. We already have a big fucking problem. So if you wanna arrest me, do it now!"

"All right, Sam! All right!"

"Please—leave us to do our work," Sam shouted. "Please don't threaten me and don't threaten them. We have work to do."

"All right," Ford growled. "You were never here."

Sam shook his head. "No. I was here. I followed this bug here. I've always been here. Remember that."

No one had been near Rudy Alvarez' pet shop since he had collapsed the day before. Whoever turned out the lights and locked the door had decided that duty ended there—the radio was still playing and the floor was scattered with the corpses of the tropical fish along with a thick carpet of heavy glass fragments from the shattered fish tanks. Robby added to it by smashing the glass of the front door, reaching in gingerly to unlatch the catch on the lock.

Robby and Lisa Aronson crept into the store, their helmets muting the whining and barking of the unfed dogs and cats in the cages that lined the wall.

"Poor things," said Aronson.

"Don't touch them," Robby cautioned.

"We'll have to get all of these animals out of here," said Aronson. "Any one of them could be infected. We'll have to test them all. Could a domestic cat or dog be the host?"

"No," said Robby. She was a few feet ahead of her colleague. All of the animals were hungry and not a little panicked, but Robby had been working with lab animals long enough to see that they looked more or less healthy. Then her eyes settled on the rhesus monkey. The animal was listless and its fur was matted and dirty. "Here's the host," she said. "And she's sick."

Lisa and Robby exchanged a look. They both knew what that meant.

"Let's get her back to the lab," said Aronson.

The rhesus monkey hardly stirred as they cautiously carried the cage out to their Hummer. Both were prepared to drop the cage if the monkey moved at all—a bite would be fatal. But the animal was too weak to defend itself and remained curled in the corner of the cage.

Back at the BL-4 lab the elation over the finding of the host was fleeting. It only took Salt a few moments to draw a syringe full of blood, to make a slide and get it under the lens of his microscope. Sam, Casey, and Robby crowded around him, waiting anxiously for the verdict. If the rhesus was the host creature then they would be able to identify it and develop an antiserum from the blood and tissue.

Salt didn't look up from the microscope. "It's the original strain. No antibodies, nothing. It's Motaba, but it's not new, improved Motaba . . ."

There was a moment of silence and the frustration in the room was almost palpable.

"He was infected earlier then," said Sam. "And yet, this one got sick before the human outbreak. How is that possible." He looked around the room. "Anybody here have any theories on that one?"

Casey was the first to hazard a guess. "Maybe he was on the boat from Africa, next to the real host animal. Maybe it happened at Biotest. That seems to be the only place that it *could* have happened. Right?"

Robby shook her head. "Biotest is clean. CDC has turned the place inside and out. Every animal is accounted for and every one is Motaba negative."

"So says the CDC," Sam snapped. "I say we test them again."

"And I say my people know what they're doing," said Robby sharply.

Sam was plainly in no mood for a debate. "Test them again, goddammit. Get one of your people to Biotest—now—and turn that place inside out."

This was the old Sam Daniels, the one who yelled and screamed and demanded the impossible done in double quick time. He would push anyone hard if he needed the results, and it didn't matter to him if you happened to be his subordinate, his superior, or Mrs. Sam Daniels. Of course, it was a quid pro quo—Sam would work as hard—harder—than anyone else. And if you couldn't cut it in the team you were expected to get lost and to waste no time doing it.

Casey did his best to hide his smile. He nudged Robby in the ribs. "Just like the old days . . . Welcome back to the team, Rob."

11

Main Street, Cedar Creek

SEPTEMBER 3, 1995, 9 A.M.

Keeping the lid on Cedar Creek was becoming more and more difficult. Unable to get any information out of the U.S. Army or the health authorities, and panicked by rumors and scare stories, much of the population of Cedar Creek had decided to hit the road, to get out of town to ride out the storm elsewhere. It had never occurred to any of them that they would be prevented from leaving.

The Army had completely ringed the town

with troops and barbed wire emplacements and had cut or barricaded key roads and bridges. Helicopters flew constant passes over the town and foot patrols of heavily armed soldiers maintained a round-the-clock guard on the perimeter line.

Within the town itself, enforcing an even tighter circle, were more soldiers. These manned the checkpoints, positions which were swept by the sights of a heavy machine gun set in a nest to the side of the road. These were backed up by armor—a tank and two armor-plated Hummers were parked athwart the main street of the town.

The street was packed with traffic. Whole families and all the possessions they could carry were crammed into cars, a long, honking line of them. But no one was going anywhere.

An officer walked down the length of the traffic jam. He was dressed in a chemical warfare suit and spoke to the crowd through a bull horn.

"We're turning you around, people," he said. "Please remain calm. No one is permitted to leave the town. Anyone attempting to do so will be placed under arrest."

He continued down the street, repeating his message. He paid no attention to the weather-beaten Ford Bronco that made up part of the sad parade. Sitting behind the wheel of the Bronco was Tommy Hull; his wife Darla was next to him. In the back seat were their two children, perched on top of a haphazard pile of family belongings just thrown into the vehicle. Darla was frightened and the kids were confused and beginning to cry. They sensed that something scary was happening and when Mommy was upset, they were upset too.

"They're not gonna let us through," said Darla. "Tommy, what are we gonna do."

Tommy pounded the wheel with the heel of his hand. "We're not sick. They can't keep us here if we don't want to be here. There's laws, ya know."

"They're the law now," said his wife. Darla watched three soldiers in bizarre chemical warfare suits walk down the sidewalk of Main Street. It had once been her street, the place where she went to shop or where she took her kids to McDonald's. Now it was in the possession of an invading foreign power.

The chemware protective gear not only set the soldiers apart from the townsfolk—if there was no danger why were the soldiers dressed like that in the first place—it seemed to render them inhuman, alien. The material was a green darker than olive drab and had a faint, oily sheen to it. The helmets the soldiers wore on their heads had dark portholes for eyepieces and barrel-shaped snouts to accommodate an air purifier, and looked like an insect's proboscis.

Ahead of the Bronco, a beat-up pickup containing three men pulled out of the stalled line of traffic, turned, and came back down Main Street. The three men were all big, two of them had long, tangled beards, and all had black T-shirts stretched across capacious beer bellies. They looked like bikers, temporarily deprived of their Harleys.

The pickup slowed as it passed Tommy Hull's Bronco and the driver of the pickup and Tommy Hull happened to make eye contact. In an instant, each knew what the other was thinking: that this whole situation was a crock, it was unfair, it was un-American—and that they should make a run for it.

"Follow us," the driver shouted.

The line of Tommy's jaw set and he made his decision, slamming his car into gear. "There ain't no law, not anymore," he said. "Get down kids." He threw the Bronco into a tight U-turn and followed the pickup down the street. The far end was blocked, but the pickup turned to the right, Tommy Hull was right behind it. Darla and the kids held on, terrified as Tommy raced to keep up with the leader.

The two vehicles were racing directly toward the second inner perimeter roadblock. Tommy's view was partially blocked by the wide bed of the pickup in front of him, but he could see soldiers running into position and he could imagine the force of the firepower they were going to face if they tried to break through that barricade. He knew he couldn't bring himself to put his kids in danger like that. . . .

Tommy lessened the pressure on the accelerator, slowing down for an instant—until he saw that the pickup wasn't going to try to run through the roadblock. Instead, the truck made a hard left, ripped through a fence and zoomed down a dirt path into an open field. Tommy followed, terrified but determined.

Suddenly there were three Hummers on their tails and all three had machine guns mounted on the roof of the armored cabs. The instant they appeared one of the men in the pickup emerged from the sunroof, a shotgun in his hands. Over the roar of his engine, Tommy couldn't hear the blasts, but he could see two puffs of blue-gray smoke as the guy discharged both barrels at the soldiers.

"Tommy!" Darla screamed. The kids were wailing. "Tommy, stop! They're crazy! They're going to—"

The rest of her words were lost in the fearsome roar of an aircraft engine. A Huey gunship passed overhead, so low off the ground the skids seemed to nick the cab of the Bronco. Tommy could see the soldier manning the .50 Cal machine gun on the door quite clearly. His face was obscured by his chemware helmet. He looked like a killing machine.

Within the chopper, however, the pilot and gunner felt sick at what was happening here—neither of them wanted this to be happening.

"Dammit, people—" muttered the gunner. "There's no place to go, don't you see that?" He stalled a moment, hoping that the drivers would come to their senses, then he fired a warning blast in front of the lead truck. But the men in the pickup were undaunted, returning fire with their shotguns.

"They'll kill us, Tommy," yelled Darla.

"They can't do that—we've got kids." But he knew they would kill them if they had to. He slammed on the brakes and the Bronco skidded to a stop in a cloud of dust. Tommy and Darla watched, openmouthed, as the helicopter swung into firing position.

There was another shotgun blast from the pickup. In the cockpit of the helicopter, the pilot and gunner heard the rattle of buckshot, clattering on the armored skin of the cabin. The pellets didn't even scratch the paint.

"What the hell are they doing?" demanded the gunner.

The pickup was racing for the cover of a stand of trees. If they made it, there was a chance they could escape. "We can't let them through," said the pilot.

"I know." The gunner turned and took aim with great reluctance. He cocked the weapon and fired. Bullets raked the pickup, the big shells shredding the flimsy metal. The driver was killed instantly and the truck careened out of control. It flipped, skidded on its roof and then erupted in flame.

The gunner felt sick. "Shit . . ." The chopper crossed over the scene, turned, and came back for another look.

Tommy and Darla stared, horrified at the burning truck, scarcely noticing that their Bronco had been surrounded by the Hummer and a squad of soldiers.

The United States Army could close down the town, but it couldn't keep their activities secret for long. By the time the second day of the quarantine dawned, news vans and reporters from countless media outlets had formed a third perimeter barrier around Cedar Creek.

The military authorities had decreed that no one could approach more than a mile from the outermost boundary, so it was there, far from the action that the reporters camped and waited for something to report on, something to photograph—something other than the nearly continuous stream of military traffic into the town.

The air space lock down was rigidly enforced, of course, and the hastily appointed army public information officer, offered no information at all, save to say, at a daily briefing, that the situation was under control and that the Army was dealing with the situation. As the siege of Cedar Creek dragged on, he became quite adept at finding different ways to say the same thing over and over again.

There was no information within the town either. Those residents of Cedar Creek who turned on their televisions in hopes of getting some information from the outside world found that the press, bivouacked a mile from their doors, had only one story to report—the lack of information.

Yet, in the Mauldin household, on a quiet street in Cedar Creek, the television ran constantly and whenever a news bulletin came on, Sherry and Mack and their three small children gathered to watch it.

"The military have escalated the quarantine of Cedar Creek," a male television reporter intoned, "thereby doubling their presence in the small town . . ."

"That's just great," grumbled Mack Mauldin, Sherry's husband.

"Authorities remain silent about numbers and details, continuing the media blackout," the reporter continued. "Sources have numbered the dead from as low as ten and as high as fifty."

"Fifty," said Sherry, horrorstruck. "Mack, how can it be fifty already?"

"They're lying," said Mack. "Pay no attention to this."

The reporter looked straight into the camera. "We can only imagine the fear and frustration of the citizens of this once very quiet rural town . . ."

Mack spoke to the screen. "I doubt it, pal."

"The population is apparently trapped, unable to move beyond the well-defined perimeters of the quarantine. Their voices too are silent to us as all phone communications have been cut off. They cannot speak to us; we cannot hear them. Those we can hear—those with the information—will not speak. It is, in a word, frightening . . ."

As the reporter signed off, Sherry coughed. She looked at her husband, worried.

"You don't have it," said Mack quickly. "Trust me, you don't have it."

"Are you sick, Mommy?" her daughter asked. Her voice was small and troubled.

Sherry did her best to smile. "No. No. Mommy's okay . . ."

A loud, amplified voice echoed from the street. "Stay inside your houses . . ."

The Mauldins went to the window of the living room and saw a Hummer with loudspeakers attached to the roof slowly rolling down the street. "There is no need to be alarmed. The situation is under control, but your cooperation is necessary to keep it that way. Repeat: there is no need for alarm . . ."

In spite of this soothing pronouncement, people were alarmed and the situation was not under control. All over the town, there had been sporadic outbursts of violence, attacks on soldiers that had been quickly and ruthlessly suppressed.

The order had gone out to herd all of the people back to their houses, even those who had been camped on the steps of the hospital waiting for news of their loved ones inside. As Sam watched the soldiers move the crowd along, a pair of trucks pulled into the parking lot and pulled up to the loading dock. Soldiers immediately got busy off-loading heavy pallets, drug boxes labeled E-1101.

"What's this?" Sam asked one of the soldiers.

"Dunno, sir."

"Where did it come from?"

"General Ford's orders, sir."

Sam turned and walked back into the hospital. Already nurses and orderlies were fanning out through the wards, hooking up bags of the mysterious E-1101 to the intravenous ports of the stricken patients.

He found Ford sitting at the bedside of Corrine, a bag of E-1101 hanging from her IV pole. Corrine was in a coma, the final stage of the disease.

"Billy?" said Sam.

Ford turned and looked at him, then turned back to Corrine. "She was one of the first ones infected . . ."

"Her name is Corrine," said Sam. He tapped the plastic bag. "What is this, Billy?"

"It's an experimental antiserum from Yale virology," said Ford. "I figured it was worth a try—" The general shrugged. "Let's see what happens."

"C'mon, Billy, I read the journals. And I haven't read a word about E-1101 . . . Where'd you get it, Billy. You know I can call Yale in a second."

"I want to save these people, Sam. Just like you. I'm using everything in our arsenal. We've got to work together on this thing."

"Are we, Billy?" Sam asked. "Are we working together?"

Ford said nothing, looking back at Corrine. She had stopped breathing—the E-1101, whatever it was, had not been the miracle drug that would save her. Ford stood and shook his head, not meeting Sam's gaze.

"Sam . . ." he said slowly. "Don't waste your time making any phone calls to Yale."

Sam disconnected the E-1101 serum from Corrine's IV and carried it outside to the BL-4 lab, handing the bag of milky brown liquid to Salt.

"Give this to the rhesus," said Sam. "Might as well see what happens."

Salt took the bag of serum, but looked perplexed. "What is this?"

"I have no idea," said Sam with a slow shake of his head. Both men looked to the monkey, who still lay listless in his cage. "Maybe he can tell us . . ."

12

Cedar Creek, California

SEPTEMBER 5, 1995

It had become known as Radio Cedar Creek and it was inescapable. The military authorities had activated the Emergency Broadcast System for the Cedar Creek district and it played twenty-four hours a day, alternately broadcasting stern warnings which always seemed to be followed by a bland message of reassurance. If you didn't have a radio or if you chose to turn it off, the Army was one step ahead. Loudspeakers transmitting the bulletins had been erected all over the town, providing a nonstop accompaniment to the squads of chemware-clad soldiers who patrolled the streets. The radio broadcasts worried the townsfolk and they were driving the soldiers crazy.

"If you're feeling sick in any way," the voice intoned, "you should hang a pillow case or any piece of white cloth on your front door. Soldiers will take you to a medical facility for a test and you will know the results within a few hours . . ."

A foot patrol crept through the streets, searching for those breaking the twenty-four-hour curfew. Around noon, they nabbed an old lady who was trying to creep into a church. They led her away sobbing that she just wanted a chance to pray.

Another patrol checked out a supermarket on the edge of town where there had been reports of looting. They found a broken front door and some pilferage, but no sign of the raiders.

The loudspeaker in the supermarket parking lot continued to blare. "Early signs resemble a flu—cough, fever, headache. Anybody showing these signs should report them immediately, as indicated . . ."

The broadcast was muted in the hospital itself, but it could be heard. "The disease is serious, but not lethal." Tracy and most of the other patrons infected at the movie theater lay dead in their beds, the sheer number of corpses to be dealt with slowing down the removal system.

"It is important that we all try to remain calm. Doctors have the situation well in hand . . ." Dr. Mascelli had enough strength left to smile weakly, then he closed his eyes and rested his head on his pillow. The first symptoms of the disease had come on him the day before and he was rapidly approaching the physical breakdown of stage two Motaba.

"Authorities are working day and night to find a cure. But if you do test positive, you'll need to go into a designated isolation unit . . ."

In the Hull household, Darla and her children listened to the radio obsessively while Tommy, her husband, worked on depleting the supply of beer stored in the garage.

"You must bring any clothes or personal things you might need."

"Yeah," said Tommy bitterly. "Real personal. Like a fucking body bag."

"They're doctors," said Darla. "They wouldn't lie. And don't talk like that in front of the kids."

"Doctors," said Tommy with a derisive snort. "They're the goddamn government, Darla. The military, for chrissake."

The kids gathered close to their mother, as if they remained with her no harm could ever befall them. Tommy crushed his beer can.

"Once again, it is important to remain calm, to trust the people who are helping us, to refrain from any sort of violent action that might put your life and the lives of others in jeopardy . . ."

Before the announcer finished his spiel, Tommy hurled the beer can. It hit the radio and sent it flying, the cheap plastic shell shattering as it hit the floor. Batteries rolled across the floor. Darla just shook her head and the kids looked to their father with frightened eyes.

"Shoulda left when we had the chance," said Tommy.

They were more law-abiding in the Mauldin house. Sherry had been trying to suppress her cough for almost a day now, but she had to admit to herself that she was sick. She felt the fever creep over her and the headache followed shortly after. Mack had known what was going on, but he felt that it was his wife's decision as to what she wanted done. Sherry bowed to the inevitable and herself hung the old beach towel on the brass knob of their front door.

Before long, they heard a truck stop in front of the house and a knock came at the door.

"I'll be back in a few hours," said Sherry, trying to muster a smile. "The doctors just have to do a little test, that's all."

Mack looked at her, holding back tears. "Don't worry about us," he managed to say.

"I might have to stay overnight. If I do, you guys gotta be good. No fighting, okay? You do what Daddy tells you." She started to kneel to kiss her children, but then thought the better of it, standing up and turning to the door. She would forgo her farewell if it meant not contaminating them.

Mack and the kids watched the soldiers lead Sherry down the flagstone walk to the waiting Hummer. It was all she could do to fight the urge to look back, wondering if she would ever see her husband and children again.

She climbed into the vehicle without a word, the chemsuited soldiers getting in behind her. The Hummer moved down the street, passing house after house, almost every door displaying towels, T-shirts, pillow cases—the pale, commonplace flags of infection. Sherry saw them and broke down, crying bitter tears for her dying world.

Portable BL-4 Lab
Cedar Creek, California

SEPTEMBER 5, 1995

The testing area of the BL-4 lab could contain about a dozen people at a time, those showing symptoms—Sherry Mauldin among them—sitting quietly in a row while medical workers in their Racal suits took blood samples. It was calm, it was quiet, and it seemed to those who had to be there as bad as purgatory, souls waiting to be judged, to find out if they are one of those damned to the disease or miraculously spared.

Lisa Aronson tightened a tourniquet of rubber tubing around Sherry Mauldin's bicep. "Make a fist, please."

Sherry curled her fingers tightly and the vein in her arm swelled and pulsed. Aronson speared it expertly with the needle of a disposable syringe and drew a draft of blood into the cylinder. Sherry hardly felt the pinch of the needle. She watched transfixed as her blood flowed. It looked quite ordinary and she was not quite able to believe that the red liquid could contain a tiny organism which would make her sick or even kill her.

Lisa Aronson capped the needle, placed a wad of gauze and bandage in the crook of Sherry's arm, and then folded back her forearm.

"You sit tight," she said. "We'll have the results in a jiffy, okay?"

Sherry nodded and watched as Lisa decanted her blood into a test tube and marked it with a grease pencil. Sherry Mauldin ceased to be Sherry Mauldin and became, as far as BL-4 was concerned, a number—612.

In the laboratory beyond the testing room Casey Schuler and Robby Keough were working as fast as they could to test every blood sample they received. It was a simple procedure. First a drop of PCR Primer was dropped into every test tube containing a blood specimen, then the mixture was worked onto a slide and put under the microscope.

Casey scarcely glanced at the sample. All he had to see was the tangle of angry viral snakes to know what he had.

"Positive."

Quickly, he selected the next slide and examined it quickly. "Positive. Dammit."

Robby looked into her own scope. "Positive."

The two doctors were working by rote, as mechanical as workers on an assembly line.

"Positive," Casey repeated. "The whole fucking town is infected."

He seized the next specimen and put it under for examination, glancing through the lens. *"Positive,"* he said angrily. He took it from the scope and placed it in the rack. It was numbered 612.

Fifty people had gone in for testing that morning and fifty had tested positive. The news was broken to them briskly, efficiently, and with the minimum of fuss by a nurse from the hospital staff. All accepted it with hardly a murmur. They were too stunned to speak at that moment; later as the awful reality sunk in, there would be more anguish, but at that moment they were so dazed by the news they allowed themselves to be led to the containment facility.

They formed into a ragged line and were herded through the hospital under the escort of a platoon of soldiers. The new cases stumbled along, walking the corridor of the hospital. The wards were filled to the walls and the overflow cases were parked in the hallway, lying on a makeshift collection of beds from the hospital and cots supplied by the Army.

It was the first time any of the new arrivals had seen the disease. Bloodshot eyes and faces crisscrossed with lesions looked up at them, moans and coughs filling the air. Sherry stopped and gaped at one, a man, his face so mottled with abrasions as to be unrecognizable. Her eyes widened in horror and her hand went to her mouth.

"Keep moving please," said a soldier, gently pushing her down the corridor. "This way . . . You will be assigned to a bed. Keep moving please . . ."

The column was guided out of the hospital, into the fresh air and sunshine. She felt a little better to be out of the close and sickening atmosphere of the hospital—until she saw the tent city.

Soldiers had worked all night erecting tent after tent, hundreds of them, all arranged in neat rows, the canvas flaps stirring in the breeze. This was the new isolation ward, it was ringed by a perimeter fence of razor wire six feet high and was guarded by dozens of soldiers, all of them dressed in their safety suits.

"Oh my God," whispered Sherry as she stared at her new home. If the test lab had been purgatory, then this, surely, was hell.

**The White House
Washington, D.C.**

SEPTEMBER 5, 1995, 6 P.M.

The political repercussions of the Cedar Creek incident were considerable and they were the responsibility of J. Thomas McCarthy, the cantankerous, hard-nosed White House Chief of Staff. The President was out of the country and he had thrown the whole mess into McCarthy's lap—and McCarthy was not happy about it. But he knew what he had to do. He read the situation reports from the field, the medical analyses from the CDC and USAMRIID, and the details of McClintock's apocalyptic Operation Clean Sweep. He hated the whole thing—particularly Clean Sweep.

McCarthy ordered a meeting for the White House situation room but before it was convened he summoned the Chief White House Counsel, the venerable and courtly Judge Toller. The two men were exact opposites. McCarthy was a tough, brazen, foul-mouthed New Yorker; Toller a soft-spoken, polished Southerner. They worked well together.

McCarthy sketched in the details of the Cedar Creek incident. Toller hardly raised an eyebrow. "Look, Judge, we're being rat-fucked here. But they tell us there is no time, no choice, but one."

Toller nodded. "Whatever we do, we must protect the President and make sure his decision is defensible."

"We've been working on this shit for fifty years," said McCarthy angrily. "Those Pentagon fucks swear they know nothing about this virus. I'll bet my right nut in a vise that's a crock of shit." He glanced at his watch. "Okay . . . It's meeting time."

The grandees of American public life gathered in the situation room of the White House to hear General McClintock's briefing on the situation in Cedar Creek. The five joint chiefs were there, as were members of the Cabinet and the majority and minority leaders of both houses of Congress.

McClintock finished his briefing exactly thirty minutes after he began it. Speaking without notes, but with some well-placed visual aids—including some gruesome footage of Motaba-ravaged bodies both in the United States and in Africa—McClintock had discoursed dispassionately and with apparent disinterest. It appeared that he had no opinion in the matter of containment of the outbreak, that he was nothing more than a dutiful servant reporting on a bad situation. Yet, at the conclusion of his talk most of the people in the room were thinking just the way McClintock wanted them to. The horror of what was going on in a small town in California told them that the outbreak of Motaba had to be contained at all costs.

"This threat," McClintock concluded, "requires the initiation of Operation Clean Sweep to eradicate the disease." There were gasps and murmurs around the room, a low buzz of concern and consternation.

McCarthy was the first to respond. He alone looked singularly unmoved by McClintock's presentation. "Thank you, General McClintock," he said. "Let me recap. The President's ETA from the Far East economic summit is about twenty hours. By then he wants a recommendation from this group."

"All due respect, Mr. McCarthy," said McClintock, "but we can't afford a day's delay."

McCarthy was neither intimidated nor dazzled by the military—unlike some people on Capital Hill. He knew too well that the disinterest of the military was often a mask for their own agenda. "General, it's a little much to ask the American people to understand the American president wasn't even in the country when an American town was being blown away. We're talking about killing thousands of American citizens."

"You're playing politics!" McClintock shot back. "People all over the West Coast could be dying tomorrow because you're worried about how the President looks."

"General, that is about enough out of you . . ." McCarthy looked around the room. "Now let's cut to the chase. What we're talking about here is firebombing the town of Cedar Creek, California. Population twenty-six hundred. With something called a fuel air bomb—the most powerful nonnuclear weapon we have. It explodes and sucks in all the surrounding oxygen to feed the core—vaporizes everything within a mile of ground zero. Men, women, children and, lucky for us, one airborne virus. Destruction guaranteed, crisis over, case closed."

McCarthy paused for a moment to let his words sink in. Then he tossed a small blue-jacketed booklet onto the table. "This is the Constitution," he said. "I've read it cover to cover and nowhere does it authorize the President to vaporize twenty-six hundred American citizens. It does say no person shall be deprived of life or liberty without due process." McCarthy shrugged. "I guess that's cold comfort for the citizens of Cedar Creek . . ."

McCarthy's eyes swept the room and settled on the only woman in the room. "I'm sure as Attorney General you and that gaggle of whiz kids over at Justice will be able to find some legal precedent that will allow the President to launch a surprise attack on sleeping American citizenry."

McCarthy was against it, but he knew there was little he could do—except to try and manage the damage. "The President will bite the bullet on this one, but what isn't going to fly is some Rose Garden press conference the next day where the President explains how in between brushing his teeth and taking a leak he decided to vaporize Cedar Creek just because a few experts recommended it or on the advice of some fucking general no one ever heard of, or after he polled half a dozen scientists and the vote was 4 to 2 in favor."

McCarthy stood and walked around the table. "So," he said, "two preconditions must be met before consideration can even be given to Operation Clean Sweep. First, there will be unanimous and unwavering support from every single person in this room and you will do it publicly." There was no doubt that McCarthy's words were being addressed primarily to the opposition members in the room—if the polls went the wrong way, they would be the first to denounce the President and make considerable political hay from the fallout.

"You're going to stand shoulder to shoulder with the President on this one. Second, you're going to get an army of experts in white lab coats citing hundreds of thousands of experiments telling every idiot with a camera that there was no other choice. Nobody from the Cabinet is going to leak to the *Washington Post* how they were really opposed and I don't want to see some pencil-necked geek in a lab coat on *Nightline* telling me how it wasn't really necessary to vaporize twenty-six hundred innocent Americans, that there was a kinder, gentler way. Understand?" McCarthy dug a fat folder out of his briefcase. "Okay, the President ordered a data package on Cedar Creek."

He tossed the file down. A sheaf of photographs skittered across the smooth wood of the tabletop. "Photographs. Faces of the people of Cedar Creek. Children, couples, young families. Read their names. Memorize their faces. These aren't Pentagon statistics. They're flesh and blood. And they are pictures that will haunt us till the day we die."

McCarthy had said his piece. He stormed out of the room, leaving a stunned silence behind him. McClintock merely rolled his eyes.

13

**Biotest Animal Holding Facility
San Jose, California**

SEPTEMBER 5, 1995

It took less than an hour to fly Dr. Julio Ruiz by helicopter from Cedar Creek to San Jose, but it took a lot longer than that for him to go item by item through the entire inventory of animals that had passed through Biotest in the last two weeks. The company president, a middle-aged man named Felder, dogged him every step of the way, insisting that he ran a clean operation. He did not make Ruiz' job any easier.

Nevertheless, when Julio Ruiz finished, he pried a fresh copy of the fourteen-day list out of Mr. Felder and checked it again. Sam Daniels' reputation for obsessive thoroughness had preceded him.

When he was certain that the manifests checked out he called Sam, reaching him in the office of the BL-4 lab.

"No animals have been removed from here for the last fourteen days," Ruiz reported. "I've double-checked the storage lists, the manifests, the vet profiles . . . Sam, I've checked every piece of paper in this whole damn place."

Felder stood in the background. "Jimbo Scott was an honest, hardworking employee," he said indignantly. "I hired him. I knew him. When you work with someone you get to know them and I knew Jimbo. Believe me."

Sam and Casey listened on the speaker phone. "Triple-check them," Sam ordered curtly. "Quadruple-check. Talk to every employee. Somebody's got to know something. The source of the whole thing was there."

"Sam—"

"The host was there, goddammit." Sam broke the connection and then slumped forward on his desk. He was exhausted, frustrated, disheartened. He picked up a styrofoam cup filled with cold coffee and sipped it. "Did you hear what he said? He said he talked to everybody there. He didn't talk to everyone there—" He grimaced. "This coffee sucks."

"Sam," said Casey gently, "maybe you should try to get some sleep."

"I don't need sleep," Sam replied. He took another sip of coffee and grimaced, as if he were realizing what it tasted like for the first time. "Casey, *you* get some sleep."

"I got some sleep," Casey replied. "Back in July."

"I have work to do," said Sam. "Don't tell me when I need sleep. I don't tell you when you need sleep."

"You just did," said Casey.

Casey left Sam sitting at his desk. He

hardly stirred, staring at the mess of notes in front of him, the tree of death, the PCR analyses, the morbidity, and mortality reports . . . None of it seemed to make sense. The figures swam before his eyes and the couch in his cramped office suddenly looked as enticing as an oasis in a desert. . . .

Sam collapsed onto the couch and fell asleep in seconds, sleeping so soundly he scarcely moved. In the lab beyond his office Robby and Casey continued to test blood sample slides, despite the fact that both of them were worn down with fatigue. More than once Casey almost nodded off over his microscope, but he caught himself, laboriously dragging himself back from the edge of unconsciousness. He blinked and shook his head, then threw his arms out and stretched, working the kinks in his neck then bent once again to his task.

A second later a bolt of fear shot through him like an electrical charge. His air hose had come uncoupled from his suit and was lying on the floor—it must have slipped out when he stretched. Frantically, he grabbed the tube and reinserted it. He was trembling inside his suit, panicked that he had breathed in the disease.

On impulse, Casey ran from the room, his umbilical cord tracking dangerously fast along the ceiling as he plunged into the sanitary air lock. He waited for the poisoned air to be sucked out, then raced into the decontamination chamber, frantically stripping off his suit as he went.

Casey threw himself under the shower, yanked on the chain, and doused himself with a great flood of green formaldehyde disinfectant. He shivered under the deluge of the cold, bitter liquid, racked more by fear than by cold. He stood under the spray for five full minutes although he knew any microorganisms he carried would have been killed in the initial onslaught, then he took a towel and sat down on the bench, worried sick.

That's how Robby found him, hunched on the bench, still shaking.

"What happened, Case?"

"Nothing," he said, trying to laugh it off. "Just suddenly got the willies. Strange, huh?"

"Nothing is strange. Not here and now . . . Why don't you get some rest. I can finish up."

"No," he insisted. "I'm fine. I *hate* them willies. They should call 'em 'the Sams,' don't ya think?"

People continued to die at an alarming rate, leaves falling from the tree of death. In the depths of the night a special squad of soldiers stole through the hospital, removing the newly dead from their beds, zipping them into body bags and hauling them out into the parking lot, stacking the dead bodies on the cold tarmac.

That night the harvest of cadavers was large—a hundred or more—and it took a long while to load all of them into the back of a heavy truck. It was backbreaking and nerve-racking labor. The dead weight of the bodies was difficult to handle and the awkward chemware suits made the arduous chore even harder. Furthermore, the soldiers knew the risks—handling cadavers infused with the dread disease meant that they had to stay alert and vigilant at all times.

Once loaded with its ghastly cargo, an MP on a motorcycle lead the truck out of the parking lot, driving through the night, passing the command center and on to the outskirts of town. There the little convoy turned off the road and drove across a field, stopping in front of a desolate, rundown wooden barn.

Pending the arrival of an army cremation unit, the military had commandeered this structure for use in disposing of the bodies. Getting rid of the contaminated corpses was a high priority for the command—allowing bodies, fertile breeding grounds for the disease, to pile up was one sure way of making sure that the epidemic would mutate and spread.

The process of unloading was just as difficult and another couple of hours passed before all of the corpses had been transferred into the barn. Next, the soldiers doused the cadavers and the old beams of the barn with gallon after gallon of gasoline, then the barn and its ghoulish contents were set alight.

Flames and black smoke spiraled into the air, the brightest light for miles around, illuminating the dark night.

Santa Rosa, California

SEPTEMBER 6, 1995, 1:15 A.M.

The monkey was hungry again. She had forsaken the campground at dawn, hiding herself in the forest during the daylight hours, venturing out at night in her endless forage for food. She could not find her way back to the campsite, stumbling instead on a small house situated on the edge of a development, on the cusp, where the forest gave way to the green carpet of suburban lawns.

The house was lit by a single, dim porch light. Hungry and curious she crept out of the forest, across the patch of grass, and scrambled up on to the porch. There was a window a few feet above the floor and the monkey jumped up onto the sill and peered through the window.

The faint light only just illuminated the room within, the room of a child. There were toys scattered about on the floor and, in the narrow bed, a small child, a little girl, could be seen curled under the covers. Her face was tranquil in slumber.

But then she opened her eyes, as if urged awake by the animal at the window. The little girl sat up in the bed and looked to the window, but whatever had roused her was gone, the monkey having bolted from its perch the instant the little girl stirred. The child stared for a moment and then lay down again, returning to her sleep and her dreams.

Cedar Creek, California

SEPTEMBER 6, 1995, 1:17 A.M.

The column of smoke and fire from the burning barn made an excellent beacon. The pilot in the helicopter navigated the aircraft by the bright light, bringing the aircraft down for a perfect landing on the helipad near the command center.

A few moments after touching down, the side door of the chopper slid open and McClintock, flanked by a couple of aides, emerged and looked around him. Then he strode toward the blockhouse and entered, the armored door closing behind him with a hiss.

McClintock found Ford hunched over his computer, staring at the data assembled there. There was a graphic, a map of Cedar Creek, and a paragraph of information, the running tally of cases of Motaba in the town: the number testing positive, the number showing stage one symptoms, those more advanced, and the number of dead. In just a few lines, the computer had outlined the death of a town.

"Evening, Billy," said McClintock. He dropped into a chair facing the desk and pulled a cigar from his breast pocket. "Some kind of operation, huh?"

The general did not seem surprised to see McClintock. In the back of his mind he knew he would show up eventually. "It's not an operation," said Ford wearily. "It's a catastrophe."

"Aw, don't take it so hard." McClintock neatly bit the end off of his cigar. "It's not your fault that this happened. I don't think it's anyone's fault."

Ford leaned back in his chair. "Donny, do you remember 1918?"

" 'Fraid that was before my time, Billy." He patted his pockets looking for matches.

"But you know your history . . . That was the year the great Spanish influenza pandemic started. Circled the globe and killed twenty-five million people in nine months."

McClintock lit his cigar and exhaled a vast cloud of smooth, sweet bluish smoke. "Yeah, I remember. My father lost three brothers in that. So? What are you getting at?"

"Well . . . let's suppose there were men

back then who could have stopped it? Only they didn't." He regarded McClintock critically for a moment. "How do you think history would have judged such men?"

McClintock took the cigar out of his mouth and looked at it intently, as if the answer to the question were inscribed on the outer leaf.

"Baloney. FDR stopped Stillwell going into Indochina and caused the Vietnam War. What did history say about him? Churchill broke the enigma code and still let the Nazis bomb the shit out of Coventry. What did history say about him? Truman dropped the bomb on the Japanese and saved hundreds of thousands of American lives and now the revisionist historians say he did it just to scare the Russians. C'mon, gimme a break . . ."

"Those men were at war," said Ford. "We are not."

McClintock shook his head. "We are at war. Everybody is at war. You wanna know about history. They asked Chou En-lai, brilliant Chou En-lai, Mao Tse-tung's Chou En-lai what he considered the effect of the French Revolution. Know what he said? 'It's too soon to tell.' " McClintock laughed. "You're not worried about history, you're worried about the media. I have a presidential green light on Operation Clean Sweep and I am going forward." He stuck his cigar in his mouth and puffed.

Ford couldn't quite believe what he was hearing. "The people in this town are Americans."

"Twenty-six hundred dead or dying Americans and if this bug gets out of there, two hundred sixty million Americans will be dead or dying." The fat cigar stuck straight out of his mouth like the barrel of a field piece and he spoke around it as if it were cemented between his big white teeth.

"What if your wife was down there?" Ford asked slowly. "What if Emma was in that town?"

"I'd be devastated," said McClintock. "Devastated." Then he grinned. "I'd have to hire a new cook. C'mon, Billy. Those people are casualties of war. I'd give them all a medal if I could, but they are casualties of war."

Biotest Animal Holding Facility
San Jose, California

SEPTEMBER 6, 1995, 9:00 A.M.

Julio Ruiz had taken over Felder's office and was interviewing every Biotest employee, trying to find out if anything—anything at all—had happened in the last two weeks that they considered out of the ordinary. He had spoken to a dozen workers already that morning and not one had anything to report.

The thirteenth employee was Neal, the security guard Jimbo Scott had bribed. He was visibly nervous when he came into the room, guilt written all over his face. He had been dreading this moment for days. He figured he was going to lose his job for sure. . . .

BL-4 Lab
Cedar Creek, California

SEPTEMBER 6, 1995, 5:00 A.M.

The few hours of sleep Sam managed to snatch were not nearly enough, but it would have to do. He was still bleary-eyed and as he sat at his desk he found that the tree of death still made no sense to him. He went around and around on it, trying in his mind to pound the facts into some kind of coherent pattern.

He and Robby tried to puzzle it out, while Salt and Casey worked in the lab beyond. There was a window between the office and the lab and they could see the two of them methodically going about their business.

"Jimbo, Jimbo, Jimbo," he groaned. "How'd he get it? Maybe we're on the wrong track. Maybe Alice gave it to him."

Robby shook her head. "No—his tissue samples showed twice the viral amplification of Alice's."

"So we're stuck," said Sam angrily.

"Sam," said Robby, "we're doing everything we can . . ."

Daniels pounded the desk with his fist. "We're not. No, we're not."

"Let's just wait for the comprehensive results," said Robby. "Once we have all the information . . ."

Sam rubbed his eyes. "Robby . . . Robby . . . Can I ask you a personal question? What did you do with the dogs? You didn't put them in a kennel, did you?"

Robby stared at him balefully. "What do you think? I tied them to a tree and left a five-pound bag of dog chow nearby."

"That's what you did to me when you left."

"Let's take another look here," said Robby. She gazed at the tree of death. "Alvarez, Jimbo Scott—"

But Sam wasn't looking at the chart. He was staring into the lab, a puzzled look on his face. "Jesus," he whispered.

Robby turned. "What?"

"Look." He pointed to the cage containing the rhesus monkey. He was sitting up in his cage, still weak but it was obvious he was recovering from his illness. The serum bag was still hooked up to his IV and was continuing the feed into his arm. "Guys, guys, look at the rhesus."

"Oh my sweet Lord," said Salt. "I guess the orange juice is working."

"But that stuff doesn't work on humans," said Sam.

"No. Sam," said Robby. "It doesn't work on Cedar Creek Motaba. This monkey was infected with the original strain."

Sam brought it home. "Exactly. So you know what that means? This is no experimental antiserum," he said. "E-1011 was designed to kill African Motaba. Son of a bitch—they had it all the time!"

Suddenly he was burning mad and he looked to Casey, expecting that his junior would be sharing his outrage. But he wasn't. In fact, he didn't seem to have heard a word of the conversation. He was pale and feverish, sweating profusely behind the visor of his biosafety suit.

Sam's indignation evaporated as quickly as it had come on. "Casey?"

Salt ran to catch Casey before he fell to the floor. "He's gonna arrest!"

Sam and Salt put Casey on a gurney and ran him into the hospital, putting him into one of the beds that had been emptied just the night before.

Sam never stopped rapping out orders. "We need blood, fluids, oxygen, ice. Get it under his armpits."

A nurse rushed into the room and began packing plastic ice packs around Casey like sandbags. Lisa Aronson pounced on Casey, lacing a blood pressure cuff around his bicep.

"Pressure?" Robby demanded.

"Coming up."

"What's his temperature?"

"One-o-six," the nurse reported.

"Let's get a suction," said Sam. "We need more ice. Casey! Open your eyes. Talk to me . . . Talk to me. You've been asleep long enough. C'mon, talk to me."

The nurses ran for more ice while Robby opened a vacutainer kit to draw blood. She carefully inserted the needle in his vein and siphoned some blood into the syringe.

Sam spoke through clenched teeth. "I said open your fucking eyes, Case—you had your chance to sleep."

Casey was not famous for responding to orders, but he reacted to this one. His eyes fluttered open.

"I had a wonderful dream, Auntie Em," he said. "You were there, and you were there . . ."

"You were at a hundred and six, but we got you back."

"How many brain cells did I kill?"

"About a billion."

Casey did his best to smile. "Now I'm only as smart as you, Sam."

"Can we give him something for his sense of humor?" Sam asked.

But the crisis was not over. Casey's smile disappeared as his lips twitched uncontrollably and his whole body began to go into seizure again. Just as Robby pulled the vacutainer needle from his arm his paroxysms wrenched her hand, knocking the needle. The sharp point nicked the glove on her hand.

"Come on!" said Sam. "We need a line! Now!" He looked to Robby and saw the horrified look on her face as she stared at the tiny scratch in the latex of the glove.

"What? What's the matter, honey?"

"It didn't get past the outer glove," she said, willing it to be so. "Hold him down—get him his line."

Aronson started to hook up the intravenous feed. "Robby," she said, trying to keep her voice calm. "We'll handle this, you get a new pair of gloves." It was as low key a way she knew to tell Robby to check the cut and disinfect if need be.

Robby made for the surgery scrub room. Her hands trembling, she tore off the outer shield and examined the glove beneath. There was a cut in the finger. Robby paled and frantically stripped off the second glove, revealing the third, the innermost layer of latex. It too was cut. She pulled that off and saw, to her horror, that there was a minuscule, minute, spot of blood on the tip of her index finger.

Terrified, Robby ran to the sink and doused the spot with iodine. "Oh God . . ." She scrubbed frantically. "Jesus!" She was frightened and angry with herself at the same time.

When Sam came into the scrub room he knew in an instant what had happened.

"I was with him in the lab last night. He

took a formaldehyde shower . . . I should have known something was wrong."

"Maybe it didn't pierce the inner glove."

"Yes it did." Robby did her best to sound composed, but she was trembling.

"Lemme see, lemme see. Put some—" Sam grabbed the bottle of iodine and poured the red liquid over her hand.

Robby snatched her hand away. "I already did that! Sam!" She broke away from him and cursed. "Goddammit—I know how to work with needles. I should have waited." Her composure was breaking down, there were tears in her eyes.

Sam grabbed Robby and held her close, a clumsy attempt at consolation. But she would not allow it. "Don't. There's nothing to say."

"Yes, there is . . ." He could see Lisa Aronson standing at the door. Sam beckoned to her. "Stay with her," he said.

14

Tent City
Cedar Creek, California

SEPTEMBER 6, 1995, 9:15 A.M.

They chose Sherry Mauldin purely at random, the two men walking down the ranks of tents until they stopped in front of hers. Sherry was sitting on her army cot, her arms wrapped around herself, as if against the cold, thinking of her husband, her children, and her home. From time to time she coughed deeply and touched the lesion that had developed on her cheek, as if hoping it had vanished.

The two men in chemware suits entered her tent, the older of the two smiling at her. "How are we feeling today?"

Sherry smiled faintly, but the pain and fear remained in her eyes. "Oh, okay I guess."

"I don't want you to worry about a thing." He motioned to the man next to him. "We're just going to take a little blood. Is that okay?"

Sherry shrugged. "I guess . . ."

The man moved quickly, as if afraid she might change her mind, plunging the needle into her arm and quickly drawing the blood.

"My kids—" Sherry asked. "Are my kids okay?"

"I'm sure they are," said the older man. He had an air of authority and seemed to be in charge.

"Can you find out for certain," Sherry pleaded. "I need to know."

The man flashed a kindly, avuncular smile. "Of course, dear. What's your name?"

"Sherry," she said. "Sherry Mauldin."

"I'll find out for you, Sherry."

"They're two little girls."

"Okay."

"Thank you."

The aide had finished taking the sample. He put it in a small aluminum case, just large enough to contain one test tube.

"We've got to go now," said General Mc-Clintock, clutching the case. "I'll get news to you about your children as soon as possible. I'm sure there's nothing to worry about . . ."

Sam drove the few miles from the hospital to the command center like a man possessed. His face was tense with desperate anger. This whole thing need never have happened and it could have been stopped almost as soon as it started. That was unconscionable, the worst abuse of medical ethics he had ever heard of, the worst he could possibly imagine.

Sam gunned the Hummer up the hill, swerving to overtake a long convoy of military trucks making their way through the inner perimeter, trundling their way out of the town. He zoomed by and brought the vehicle to a halt in a shower of dust and gravel in front of the command center.

When Sam Daniels burst into the office, General Ford was on the phone. One look at Sam's face and he hung up abruptly—the desperate anger there was so intense it radiated like white hot heat.

"Yes, Sam," he said mildly.

"You knew," Sam spat. "You knew about Motaba this whole time—E-1101 was the antiserum for the original strain. You could have stopped this outbreak before it mutated. You didn't."

"We couldn't," said Ford with an apologetic shrug. He had known all along that this would come out eventually. Sam Daniels was too smart and he knew his job too well to fool for long.

"We?"

"We. That's all you need to know."

"No, Billy," said Sam. He fell forward onto the desk top. "I also need to know the host."

Ford did not reply and turned away, as if signaling the end of the interview. But Sam Daniels would not let it end there. He grabbed Ford by the shoulders as if he were a recalcitrant child. "What is the host!"

Ford shook himself free. "We never found it. We synthesized the antiserum in the lab."

"In order to protect our troops," said Sam. "Now the virus comes here . . . two kids die . . . and we could have stopped it right there but we don't . . . all to protect the perfect biological weapon. But the virus is smarter. It mutates. Now we can't stop it. We could have, but now we can't."

"The decision was made in the interest of national security," said Ford. "At the time, we thought we could accept a certain number of losses."

Sam sat down heavily. "Robby's infected," he said.

"I'm sorry," said Ford.

Sam ran a hand through his hair. "Town's dying, Casey's dying . . . and in the interests of national security, my wife is dying."

"Isn't she, in fact, your ex-wife, Sam?"

"What's your point?" Sam asked with a scowl.

"My point is your penchant for distorting

the facts. You and Robby are, in fact, divorced. You want to know who is 'we'? 'We' is you, Sam. Unless you resigned from the Army and nobody told me. You don't just do the research and it ends there. We have to defend ourselves against all the other maniacs who are developing their own biological weapons. That's the game, Sam. And you and I are part of it. Yes, it was a tragic mistake to hold back E-1101, but it's beyond that now. We've done all we can as doctors and we have to move on, as soldiers."

Sam shook his head, as if clearing it after a hard blow. "You're going to wipe out the town. You're going to eradicate the mutation. And then your weapon is intact. "It's already been ordered, hasn't it? For when, Billy? When?"

"Twenty hundred," said Ford. "By order of the President."

"The President? How?"

"He was shown the projections and carefully advised by a panel of virologists."

"I wasn't there," said Sam.

Billy Ford nodded slowly and looked at his subordinate for a long moment. "Had you been there, Sam, what would have been your advice?"

Sam was more than angry when he drove down the hill a few minutes later. He was frightened too. Hardly seeing the road, he drove frantically. The road into the town was clear—the way out was clogged with a stream of military vehicles. As he drove he tried to marshall his thoughts. Twenty hours was eight o'clock, that gave him fewer than twelve hours to mount a counter attack on the disease and the combined forces of the United States Government and the U.S. Army.

His cellular phone lying on the seat next to him rang shrilly. Sam snatched it. "What?"

It was Walter Salt. "Ruiz called. Seems he scared a security guard into telling him that Jimbo Scott smuggled an animal out of Biotest."

Sam's heart beat a little faster. This could be the break that he had promised to Robby less than an hour before—and not a moment too soon. "What kind of animal?"

"Couldn't say," Salt replied. "It was small enough to fit in the back seat of the car. Monkey. Dog. Cat. Pig. No name on the ship either, but the guard knew it was from Asia, and we have the approximate date of arrival."

"That's it?"

"That's it."

"Shit. It's something at least—may be enough. We gotta find that ship. All right, my friend, you better pack. We've got work to do." It turned out that the big break wasn't much, but it was all Sam had and he would take it.

**Command Center
Cedar Creek, California**

SEPTEMBER 6, 1995, 9:40 A.M.

When McClintock heard that Sam Daniels had been right there in Ford's office, he pounced on Briggs.

"Daniels was here?" McClintock roared. "Why was I not informed?"

"Sir," said Briggs, "you were asleep."

"I am never that asleep, Briggs. You go find him and arrest him."

"On what charges?"

McClintock did not hesitate. "Endangering national security. Where's General Ford?"

"He's in his office—" said Briggs.

"Is he asleep? It's all right. I'll wake him up." McClintock did not wait for answer. He strode toward Ford's office and threw open the door.

15

There wasn't much time, but Sam was determined to find the time to say goodbye to Robby, doing his best to try to reassure her. She was outwardly calm, but Sam knew her well enough to know that she must be in turmoil inside, torn between fear for herself and the need to go on working to contain the outbreak.

"We'll find the host," Sam told Robby solemnly. "That's a promise."

"I wish the little shit would just call in. It would make life so much easier," said Robby with a rueful smile. "Sam. Even if you do find the host, its antibodies won't fight the mutated strain. We both know this. Let's be realistic, okay?"

Sam knew all of this, of course, but there was no sense in being defeatist. However, the role of pie-eyed optimist did not come easily. "We can't be certain about that," he said slowly. "It might carry antibodies for any number of strains."

Robby smiled. "Now there's a good doctor . . . With that great bedside manner Dr. Sam Daniels is so famous for."

"Look, let's not be realistic about this thing, okay? There's a chance. Remember when you won the lottery?"

Robby looked puzzled. "I never won the lottery."

"Well, someone did . . . We've just got to hope."

"I know," said Robby. "Now go. You've got your work to do and I've got my work here. It's my job to help these people, no matter what happens. As long as I'm able to—" She broke off, feeling the catch in her throat, afraid that she would break down if she said another word.

Sam took her hand. "Robby . . ."

Salt had seen six Hummers screaming down the hill toward the hospital. He had no doubt why they were coming. He didn't want to break up this poignant moment, but he had to. "Sir, I think we should go. Very soon. Like now."

Robby found her voice again. "*Go*, Sam," she urged quietly. "I'll be all right, okay, Sam? Promise you won't worry about me?"

"Promise . . ." he said. "I'm lying. I will worry about you."

Robby smiled. "Well, yeah—you'd better."

Salt was at the window, watching as the three Hummers screeched to a halt in front of the hospital. There were four MP's in each vehicle—six rushed into the hospital and six headed for the BL-4 lab.

"Sir!" Salt insisted. "Let's move!"

"Right."

The MP's came crashing into the buildings, grabbing the first nurse they saw. "We're looking for Colonel Daniels."

"I think he's upstairs," the nurse replied.

"Which room?"

"I . . . I don't know, I can page him."

"Upstairs," the MP ordered his squad. "Move it!"

Salt and Daniels dashed into the decontamination chamber. They stripped off their Racal suits and threw themselves under the formaldehyde shower, scrubbing fast and frantically.

"How many hours of flight time?" Sam asked hurriedly.

"Sixty plus, sir."

"Actual flying time?"

Salt grinned. "Every minute, yanking and banking, sir."

"Good. Let's go."

They toweled off quickly, then almost jumped into their BDU's, running out of the room—almost smack into a squad of MP's.

The MP's did not find them, but they did find Robby. "Have you seen Colonel Daniels?"

"Colonel Daniels?" Robby asked innocently. "A big, tall blond guy with a button nose?"

"Naww, that's not him . . ."

Sam and Salt walked out of the hospital, looking as calm as they could, slung their duffel bags in the back of the Hummer, and drove away, making for the heliport. A Loach helicopter was on the pad, a squad of soldiers swarming over it, gassing it up, readying it for an outbound flight.

Daniels crooked a finger at the burly crew chief, a master sergeant, who straightened and saluted when he saw the two officers.

"What can I do for you, sir."

"Sergeant, where's your pilot? General Ford's just called from CP. We have helicopter priority to deliver flash traffic."

Salt slapped the duffel bag. "Got priority cargo."

"Where is he? The pilot," asked Sam impatiently.

The sergeant didn't hesitate. He was in no position to argue with a bird colonel and a major. "Yessir. My pilot is—"

"Your pilot is *what*, Sergeant?"

"My pilot is taking a leak, sir."

"Oh . . . shit. We'll wait in the Loach."

"Sir."

"You better tell him to shake it off!"

"Sir!"

"Why don't you go give him a hand, Sergeant!" Salt yelled.

The sergeant hurried away in search of the chopper pilot while Salt and Daniels climbed into the machine. Salt took the pilot's seat and looked at the controls.

"Look familiar?" Sam asked.

"It's like riding a bicycle, sir. Once you learn, you never forget . . . I think." He started the engine, the rotors beginning to turn slowly. Salt increased the power and felt the lift, the engine straining to pull the machine off the ground.

To the left of the pilot's seat, like the hand brake on a sports car, was a lever, the cyclic, the control that regulated the lift of the craft. Pull it up and the helicopter went up, push it down and it stayed down.

The trouble was, the movement of the cyclic had to be coordinated with the operation of the joystick that Salt held in his right hand and the twin rudders he controlled with foot petals.

"Okay," said Sam, "let's go."

"Uh-huh," said Salt uncertainly. "Right

. . ." Salt pulled up on the cyclic and back on the joystick, kicking the rudder right. The chopper lurched into the air and tipped, the rotors almost striking the ground.

"Jesus!" yelled Sam.

Panicked, Salt overcorrected and the chopper jerked to the left, then righted itself, bucking and lurching five feet above the ground.

"Stop those men!" Sam peered out the window to see the detachment of MP's rushing toward the reeling machine. The chopper heeled over again, the rotors narrowly missing the MP's, who went facedown in the dust.

The helicopter rose unsteadily into the sky, gaining altitude every second. Salt gave the engines a little more fuel and the chopper started forward, wobbling and swaying.

"How did you do in flight school, Salt?" Sam asked.

"Great, sir. It's all coming back to me . . ." The chopper tipped crazily, almost clipping a church steeple before Salt brought it back under control. "Bit by bit . . ."

"Good." Sam unzipped the duffel bag and rooted through the clothing and weaponry inside. He pulled out a map of California, unfolded it, and studied it closely.

"Get us to Oakland," Sam ordered. "Best to follow the coastline—the fog will give us some cover."

Salt swallowed hard. "Fog, sir?"

Sam continued to study the map. "There's always fog on the coast north of San Francisco, around Point Reyes."

"That a fact," said Salt with a sick little smile.

Sam Daniels looked at his pilot. "Eighty hours of flight time, Salt. You must have flown through fog, right?"

"Right . . . Well, I read about it." Salt hunkered down in the seat and gripped the controls tightly. "I can do it," he said firmly. "I can do it. I'm sure."

"Of course you can—because you read that chapter very carefully, right?"

"Absolutely!"

It fell to Colonel Briggs to break the news of the escape to Ford and McClintock. It was not a duty he relished, but he had to get it over with.

"Sirs," said Briggs, out of breath. "Colonel Daniels has just commandeered one of our choppers."

"What?" McClintock turned on Ford. "Dare I ask how? Don't waste time thinking about it, Briggs. Find him and if he resists, shoot him."

Briggs figured he had gotten off easy. "I understand, sir."

"Good."

"Wait a minute!" Ford protested. "Wait! You don't have to do this." Briggs paused at the door.

"He's a carrier." McClintock shoved Briggs on his way. "Go. Do it. Now. Do it."

"I'm doing it, sir." Briggs was gone.

"You go after him like this and the press is going to swarm all over it," said Ford. "You'll create a panic."

"Fuck the press," said McClintock.

"He's not infected," said Ford hotly. "You know that."

"I know he's been in direct contact with Motaba patients. Do you know something beyond that, Billy? You should have arrested him when you had the chance . . ."

Palisades, California

SEPTEMBER 6, 1995, 10 A.M.

Kate Jeffries had been hard at work all morning, busy with her crayons, drawing a picture for her mother. At four years old, Kate combined the relentless energy of a toddler with the seriousness of art, striving to capture in Crayola and construction paper the exact nature of her experience. It was a stick figure, a little girl with bright yellow hair holding out something to a small, black-and-white creature.

She had woken the day before with the memory of what she had seen deep in the night still fixed firm in her mind. The little girl had conducted a search of her backyard, leaving treats—bits of cookie and slices of apple—at likely points in the shrubbery on the edge of the yard. Then she waited.

The monkey emerged about midmorning, looking at the little girl for a moment, before snatching up the food and eating it quickly. Kate was amazed and delighted that the exotic animal had appeared in her backyard. She raced into the kitchen, pulled some more apple slices from the refrigerator, and quickly went outside again.

She laid down a trail of fruit up the lawn and then settled on the grass to see what would happen next. The monkey's head popped out of the undergrowth, looked at Kate, then at the line of apple slices. She seemed to be in an agony of indecision, the natural caution she felt battling her desire for the treats.

Hunger won out. Keeping a wary eye on the little girl, the monkey scuttled from her lair and grabbed the first few pieces of apple, stuffing them into her mouth until her cheeks bulged. Then she stopped, as if wondering how far she dared to push her luck.

"Come on," whispered Katie, coaxing the animal forward. "I won't hurt you . . ."

The monkey seemed to think that Kate could be trusted. Kate picked up a piece of apple and held it out in her small hand. The monkey sat on her haunches and then reached out, her leathery claw closing around the apple—for a split second, the little girl and the animal were joined by the link of a small piece of apple. They did not touch, but they had connected. . . .

This was the scene that Kate Jeffries was trying to capture in her drawing. Kate's mother looked over her daughter's shoulder as she put down a snack on the table, examining the picture.

"So this is what you've been working on all day," she said with a smile.

"Uh-huh," said Kate, nodding solemnly. "She's a monkey. Her name is Betsy."

"Betsy." She considered the name for a moment. "You're right. She looks like a Betsy," said Mrs. Jeffries finally.

"I'm feeding her, see?" said Kate. "She lives in the woods and she comes to visit me."

"Really? Tell me, honey, are there a lot of monkeys in the woods?"

Kate shook her head vigorously. "Nope. Just Betsy. I'm her only friend."

Mrs. Jeffries gave her daughter a big hug. "Does Betsy like apples like *my* monkey?" Kate giggled and gobbled down a slice of apple.

There was nothing like the imagination of a child, Mrs. Jeffries thought. Where do they get these ideas from?

**Federal Building
Oakland, California**

SEPTEMBER 6, 1995, 10:55 A.M.

Every ship that entered the Port of San Francisco-Oakland registered its cargo manifest in the Hall of Maritime Records, a cramped, airless warren of rooms in the Federal Building in downtown Oakland. There was always a line of ship agents and chandlers standing in line there to register the paperwork on behalf of the ships they represented.

Sam and Salt, looking out of place in their rumpled BDU's, stared with dismay at the long line of people separating them from the bored bureaucrat at the lone window. Daniels walked straight to the head of the line, trying to ignore the irate customers who had been waiting for some time.

"Make a hole, people," Salt shouted in his best parade ground voice.

The clerk, however, was not about to let him get away with it. "Hey, General, there's a line there you know."

"I'm Colonel Sam Daniels from USA-MRIID—"

"And I'm George from Sioux Falls, South Dakota. Back of the line, Colonel."

Sam did not have time to be polite. "We've just come from Cedar Creek."

In case he didn't get it, Salt added: "Cedar Creek, site of the viral infection!"

Sam leaned in close enough to breathe on George. "This is a bad virus, George. Need I say more? We need all the bills of lading from ships arriving from Africa in the last three months . . . now. You want me to cough on you, George?"

There had been all kinds of scare stories circulating about the killer disease that was spreading in Cedar Creek—the clerk had heard them and so had every person standing in the line. They started backing away from the two men as if the disease were emanating from them in waves.

"Uh . . . I think you need to talk to Mrs. Pananides," said the clerk.

"Fine," said Sam. "Where is she?"

"I'll get her . . . *Mrs. Pananides*," he called.

Mrs. Pananides emerged from her office. "What the hell is it, George?" She was a hefty, heavily made-up woman with a sharp look in her eye that suggested she did not suffer fools gladly.

"Uh . . ." said George nervously. "I think these men need some help."

Mrs. Pananides swung around and looked sternly at Sam and Salt. "What?"

Sam quickly explained who he was, where he had come from, and what he needed. In contrast to George and the other people in the room, Mrs. Pananides displayed absolutely no traces of fear. "Okay," she said. "Follow me."

The woman led the two soldiers into her small cubicle and turned on the printer attached to her computer. "Biotest, huh?" she said, her fingers flying over the keyboard. "You're lucky there. Biotest is very careful about their paperwork. When you're dealing with something like live cargo and federal regulations, they'd better be."

She hit the print button and the printer spat out a sheaf of paper. Mrs. Pananides ripped it off the roll and handed it to Sam. "Anything there?"

Salt and Sam compared the Biotest inventory against the maritime arrivals list. Sam read off the names of the ships while Salt found them on the inventory.

"Petra," said Sam.

"Same."

"Venus."

"Same."

"Patricia."

"Same."

"Tae Kuk . . ." Sam looked up. *"Tae Kuk—*you got it?"

"No, sir."

"It's not on the list?" Sam's heart leaped. *"Tae Kuk Seattle.* Arrived in San Francisco a week ago; one monkey, delivered to Biotest—no match on their list. This is our vessel."

They passed in a moment. The manifest marked it as already having left port. "It's already on its way back to Korea. How are we going to locate it?"

Mrs. Pananides looked at the two men, her eyes bright with the gleam of a natural conspirator. "Boys? I got me a friend in the Coast Guard. I can make a call easy."

"How close a friend?" asked Sam.

"Closer than his wife would like," said Mrs. Pananides slyly.

"That's close," said Salt. "Very close."

Salt was happy, but as the pilot in this venture, he was also looking a little further down the road. What would they actually *do* with this ship when they found it.

The Loach was in the air again heading due west from San Francisco. Mrs. Pananides' pal in the Coast Guard had told her that the last known position of the *Tae Kuk Seattle* was 127 degrees 41 feet West, 37 degrees 39 feet North. The guy at the Coast Guard said that wasn't too far out in the Pacific—about fifty miles—but once the chopper was out of sight of land, the vastness of the ocean was intimidating and the task before them suddenly seemed daunting.

Salt had activated the Loran radar, which showed their own position to within a hundred feet of accuracy and SEATEST ship-tracking radar which had located a vessel in the vicinity of the *Tae Kuk Seattle*'s last known bearings. They were making for it, moving in fast, but so was nightfall and the weather seemed to be worsening.

Sam worked the radio, calling the freighter every twenty seconds but receiving nothing in return but headphones full of static. After thirty fruitless minutes he tore them off and tossed them aside.

"Nothing. I can't raise her. Salt, you're gonna have to get us out to that ship."

"You want me to fly fifty miles over rough

seas and drop you onto a tiny freighter? With all due respect, sir, that's idiotic."

Sam grinned. "Salt, we are fugitives from the law now. Idiocy is our only option. Besides, you might serve time, but you'll have a hell of a story to tell your grandkids."

"That's such a comfort to me right now," said Salt. "You have no idea . . ."

Sam turned serious. "We've got to identify the host," he said. "Robby and Casey don't have much time . . ."

Cedar Creek Hospital
Cedar Creek, California

SEPTEMBER 6, 1995, 11:30 A.M.

Robby could feel the disease growing within her. She was achy and feverish and was beginning to weaken. The work was beginning to wear her down, ordinary movements and actions required more and more of her strength, and her eyes hurt as she peered into the microscope.

Abruptly, she got up from the lab table and went into the bathroom. She was shocked at what she saw in the mirror. Her eyes were red and watery and thin streams of blood ran from her nostrils. She had been working around disease for her entire professional life and somehow she and the other virologists had always been able to distance themselves from illness. Contagion was always something that happened to other people. . . .

"Oh Jesus," she whispered. She put her head in her hands, massaging her temples, as if trying to rub away the pounding pain in her head. The hammering seemed to be exacerbated by the loud rumbling of a dozen truck engines.

Robby glanced out the window and watched as a convoy of military vehicles moved down the street, away from the hospital. Robby had gotten used to seeing military vehicles in the streets, but it struck her that this convoy was huge, much larger than anything she had seen before. The trucks inched forward through the perimeter fence, a parade of heavy trucks streaming out of the town.

As the last truck turned the corner, leaving the street eerily empty, Robby realized what was going on. The town had been abandoned, the Army had given up and was beating a hasty retreat. For all her frustration with the United States Army, it was the only force capable of dealing with this outbreak—and now they were leaving. That could not be a good thing. . . .

The helicopter had hit heavy weather and Salt had taken the craft down as low as he dared to get under it. Things were marginally better just above wave height, but the sea was pitching and roiling as the storm descended. Sam was back on the radio trying to contact the ship.

"*Tae Kuk*—do you read? We need your exact bearings. We are U.S. Army helicopter, number—" He stopped for a moment and clicked off the microphone. "What is our registration number?"

"I have no idea."

"*Tae Kuk* . . . We need your bearings."

"It's a needle in a haystack, sir."

Sam peered into the haze of water and salt spray. A red light flashed from the superstructure of a ship. "There's our needle, Salt."

Salt looked down at the rough water. "I can't land this on that shit, sir. If I try and I don't make it we'll never get off."

Sam opened the side door and started buckling himself into the harness attached to the winch and line. "But you can get me on it, right?"

Salt and Sam exchanged a look. Both men were terrified by what they were about to do.

"Lie to me, Salt," said Sam. "Lie to me with that comforting assurance."

"Piece. Of. Cake."

They were over the ship now, Salt holding the chopper as steady as he could. Sam swallowed deep and then swung the arm of the winch out and then, with another deep gulp, followed it out into the void. He hung there for a moment.

"You say when, sir," Salt yelled.

"You're the damn pilot," Sam screamed back at him. "*You* say when."

"When?"

"Now!"

"Okay. When. Now. Sir." Salt hit the switch on the control panel that activated the winch. As Sam sank out of sight, Salt heard him shouting:

"Salt . . . You have to work on this reassurance thing."

Sam descended a lot faster than he expected to. Looking down between his feet, he could see the deck rushing up to meet him. Without thinking, he hit the release catch in the middle of the harness dropping the last eight feet to the deck. He hit hard and rolled, slamming into a metal air vent. He lay there for a moment, winded and bruised, but not broken.

Daniels staggered to his feet and looked up. The chopper was hovering just thirty or forty feet above the deck, the line and the harness fluttering and spinning in the wind. Sam gave Salt the thumbs up and then made his way unsteadily across the deck.

Just inside the first bulkhead he found the first body. An Asian man was sprawled on the deck, his face crisscrossed with Motaba lesions. Somehow Sam had expected this. He did not touch the body, but he wasn't unduly frightened of infection. Anyone on board who had died of the disease had been contaminated by the pure Motaba strain, as long as he stayed away from blood or saliva he was in the clear.

The crew's quarters were tiny, a cramped series of cabins and a picture of devastation. There were a few corpses on cots, but most were sprawled on the floor. Only one man was in bed, medicines and a thermometer on the shelf next to him. Sam figured this was patient zero, the first on board the vessel to come down with the disease and, therefore, the only one to receive any kind of care.

Pinned to the bulletin board beside the bed were Polaroid photographs, a picture of the dead seaman—and the black-and-white colobus monkey that Kate Jeffries had befriended and named Betsy.

16

Tent City
Cedar Creek, California

SEPTEMBER 6, 1995, 12 NOON

Sherry Mauldin lay on her cot, her eyes crimson red, her face pale and feverish. There were more lesions than there had been the day before. The air was alive with the moans and cries of the infected around her and in the next bed a man coughed blood continuously.

The loudspeaker crackled into life, broadcasting that same smooth, calm voice that had been on the air since the first day of the crisis. "We are pleased to announce that the crisis is abating. Military presence in the town is no longer necessary and is being scaled back, though the curfew remains in effect and will be enforced . . ."

Sherry hardly listened to the announcement. That was the voice of the military and she did not trust a word of it. She was dying, she knew that—she had seen people die around her—but the hardest thing to bear was the lack of news of her family. The man who had taken a blood sample the day before—the soldier—had never returned, brought no news of her children as he had sworn he would. His betrayal hurt her deeply.

The announcement was being transmitted throughout the town. There was practically no sign of the military except a skeleton crew of guards, all still dressed in the protective chemware suits.

"Remain in your houses," the broadcast continued. "You will be safe there. Repeat: curfew measures remain in effect and will be enforced. This is normal procedure and there is no need to be alarmed . . ."

Tommy Hull drained the last can of beer in his stash and listened to the announcement echoing eerily in the deserted streets.

"Supplies will be delivered to those who need them, and further instructions will be forthcoming. Until then, citizens are to maintain the status quo and stay where they are . . ."

"Status quo," Tommy muttered drunkenly. "Supplies . . ."

"The crisis is coming to an end . . ."

"Well, that's a load off my fucking mind," said Tommy. He lurched out of his armchair, picked up the rifle leaning against the arm, and staggered to the window. He threw it open and raised the weapon. Parked at the intersection of his street and the main road was a Hum-Vee. He squeezed off a shot and listened to the bullet flatten itself against the quarter-inch armor.

"Yo! How about a delivery, motherfuckers. I need some beer!" He fired off three shots in fast succession. "You bug-eyed bastards! Get out of my goddamned town!" He fired again, the bullet howling off into the darkness. "You lying Nazi sons of bitches! I got rights!" His next bullet hit the headlight of the vehicle, blowing it away. "You'll die before I do!"

The hatch of the Hum-Vee opened and a soldier, faceless behind his chemware mask, appeared, his M-16 aimed. Tommy Hull knew what was coming. As the bullets tore into him, a final, strangled curse died on his lips and he fell to the floor and did not move.

Getting Sam Daniels off the *Tae Kuk Seattle* had been even more difficult than landing him on it. He had stood on the forward deck, his arms in the air for almost forty-five minutes, trying to snatch the harness from the lifeline while Salt lowered the chopper as far down as he dared. Each time it looked as if he had the rig within his grasp, the chopper lurched or the ship rolled and it was pulled from his hands. Finally, in pure desperation, he made a blind lunge for the harness, grabbed it, and was abruptly yanked into the sky.

Exhausted, panting from fear and fatigue, Sam scrambled into the cockpit and lay sprawled in his seat.

"Jesus . . . I don't ever want to do that again."

"Make that two of us, sir." Without waiting for instructions, Salt turned the chopper around and was heading east toward dry land as fast as he could. "Did you find anything?"

"The entire crew is dead," said Daniels. "It must have been premutation Motaba." He dug the picture out of his pocket. "This is the face of evil, Salt."

Salt looked at the furry creature. "Cute."

"Ain't she?"

"Now what?"

"We have to get the word out."

"Any ideas how?"

"Television," said Sam.

" 'Course." Salt did not ask how Sam planned to arrange to be on television. He figured he'd find out what he had up his sleeve soon enough.

Santa Rosa, California
SEPTEMBER 6, 1995, 12:35 P.M.

They spotted the helipad on the outskirts of Santa Rosa, a large circle of concrete emblazoned with the call letters WNER and the logo of the small UHF TV station serving the Sonoma area.

"See," said Sam. "Television. Put it down there."

"You're the boss."

Sam dug two side arms out of the duffel and handed one to Salt. "You checked out on this?"

"As good as I am on choppers, sir."

"Then I've got nothing to worry about . . ."

The two soldiers scrambled out of the helicopter the instant the engines cut.

The Governor of California was holding a press conference in Sacramento and every monitor in the station was tuned to it. "The President's scientific advisors at FIMA have assured me there is no threat of the further spread of the disease at the present time—"

The TV cut to a female anchor. Behind her were photos of Sam and Salt.

"In a related story, the two men who escaped from Cedar Creek quarantine this morning, and are believed to be infected with the disease, were spotted earlier today in Oakland."

It was at that moment that Sam and Salt burst in, guns at the ready. They marched directly through the small station, bursting into the crowded news studio. On the set, two news anchors, a man and woman, saw the two soldiers enter and jumped to their feet.

"What the hell is going on?"

"Everybody, remain calm," Salt shouted. He raised his hand making sure everyone got a good look at his weapon. "Military emergency. Remain calm."

People gaped at the two men—they recognized them. In the time Sam and Salt had been in the air, McClintock had made sure that their photographs had been splashed on every television screen from Alaska to Florida, along with a lurid story: the two men were renegade officers and dangerous on two counts—they would not hesitate to kill anyone who tried to stop them and that they were infected with the Cedar Creek virus and were thus highly contagious.

Salt and Sam couldn't help but notice that

the anchors and the floor crew were looking at them as if they were walking death.

"There's nothing to worry about," said Sam. "We just need to use your TV station for minute."

A segment producer shrank away from him as if the air between them was now contaminated, deadly. "Sure, sure, whatever you say. You're the boss."

"Just keep those cameras rolling."

"You bet," he said—and he meant it. The carriers of the deadly disease may have walked into his TV station—but they had also delivered the scoop of the decade.

In the control room, the crew watched Sam and Salt walk onto the news set.

"That's them," said someone. "Those are the guys the Army is looking for."

The director, secure behind the glass in his booth, spoke into his mike, moving his cameramen around. "Two, get your camera on 'em. Two? Did you hear me?"

Sam was on the sound stage now. There was no operator on camera two, but camera one had not abandoned his post. The man looked terrified.

"We are not infected," Sam insisted. "Don't leave your camera, fella, we're not going to hurt you."

The female anchor was still rooted to her seat, gaping at Sam. He dropped into the chair next to her, picking up the lapel mike her partner had thrown there when he took off. He clipped it to the collar of his fatigues.

"Which camera do I talk to?"

The woman pointed. "That one."

"Do I talk now?"

In her earpiece she could hear the director screaming: "Yes! Yes! Tell him to start talking!"

"Anytime you're ready," said the female anchor.

Sam Daniels cleared his throat, suddenly feeling quite self-conscious. "My name is Colonel Sam Daniels," he said. "I am here with Major Salt. I expect you've heard of us, so let me say *we are not infected with the Motaba or Cedar Creek virus*, as some will have you believe. But many people are. We have identified the animal carrying the Motaba virus, and we need your help in finding it . . ." He fumbled in his pocket and pulled out the

Polaroid he had found aboard the freighter. He held up the picture. "This is the animal, a monkey . . . Here's a photo of it. Can you get a shot of it? Good. There."

Camera one moved in. Sam could see the photograph fill the monitor on the floor behind the camera. "It's a small monkey with white fur on its back. *Please* . . . do not attempt to go near it. If you see it, call the Center for Disease Control at 404-555-9653. I repeat: do not attempt to capture this animal. Just call the number. Many people are going to die unless we find it. Help us if you can."

Salt had found a piece of paper and had scrawled the number on it and held it up.

"Please," Sam continued. "This is very important. If you locate the animal tell the authorities immediately—but do not approach it. It is extremely dangerous . . ."

Mrs. Jeffries hadn't really been paying attention to the television set that was playing in her kitchen. She caught a stray word— monkey—and turned her head in time to see the photograph of the deadly animal. Her mind whirling, she looked to the refrigerator door where Kate's drawing occupied the place of honor.

The photograph was blurred and indistinct, the drawing was less than precise, but it was plain that the little black-and-white creature was the one these men were looking for.

"Kate?" Mrs. Jeffries looked around the room. Her daughter was nowhere to be seen. Frantic, she threw herself at the kitchen window, the color draining from her face as she saw Kate marching across the rear lawn, a plate of scraps clutched in her hands. . . .

"Oh my God, Kate," she whispered. Then she dashed for the door.

Santa Rosa, California

SEPTEMBER 6, 1995, 1:40 P.M.

The cops got to the television station just in time to see the Loach lift off the helipad. Half a dozen cruisers roared into the station parking lot and came to a screeching halt. Officers tumbled out of the cars, guns at the ready. They fired at the chopper, but Salt, who was definitely getting the hang of this, was roaring away, the throttles full open.

One of the cops grabbed the microphone in his cruiser. "Suspects heading northwest . . ." The helicopter jinked left and started east. "Strike that," the cop reported. "East. Suspects are now heading east . . ."

The helicopter zoomed east at treetop height, Sam screaming over the sound of the rotor to make himself heard on his cellular phone. The call had come in from the CDC, from Dr. Reynolds himself.

"Thank God that woman called," he shouted. He scanned a map of California as he spoke. "Robby? I don't know how she is. But she'll be grateful you called, Dr. Reynolds. I'll see to it that she thanks you personally."

He clicked off the phone and punched a point on the map. "We go here," he said. "Palisades."

Salt looked at the map, then looked at Sam dumbfounded. "If I heard correctly, sir. This information is coming from a little girl? A toddler?"

Sam nodded vigorously. He believed the story because it made sense—he also *wanted* to believe, more than anything he was ready for a miracle.

"Listen, Salt," he said eagerly, "this is how it unfolds. Jimbo Scott takes the monkey to Cedar Creek, right?"

"Right?"

"Something goes wrong—the pet store won't buy it. Then Jimbo flies from San Francisco to Boston, but without the animal, right?"

"Right . . ."

Sam points to the map again. "This place, Palisades, is on the way to San Francisco airport. So somewhere between Cedar Creek and the airport Jimbo ditches the monkey and it ends up in this little girl's backyard. Simple."

"If you say so, sir." He ran his eyes over the gauges on the control panel. "Fuel's low."

"I'll *piss* fuel if I have to," said Daniels.

Finally, Colonel Briggs got to deliver some good news. He ran into Ford's office and looked at the two generals triumphantly. "We intercepted a cellular phone transmission, sirs. Daniels and his sidekick are headed to a house in Palisades. They're just a few miles east of it now. I've got two teams on standby."

McClintock jumped to his feet. "Good, Briggs, a potential screwup you've managed to avoid among many others you have not. Who do you think should handle this now?"

"You, sir," said Briggs dutifully.

"You kiss ass with the best of them," said McClintock, grinning. "You hope to make general someday?"

"Yes, sir." Briggs looked hopeful.

"Well you won't." Briggs' face fell. "Get me on one of those choppers."

Briggs tried hard not to look disappointed. "Follow me, sir."

The two Hueys were on the pad, gassed and ready to go. McClintock swung into the passenger seat of the one nearest and slapped the pilot on the shoulder. "I trust you are the best helicopter pilot in this man's army."

The pilot nodded and grinned. "Yes, sir."

"Good. We're looking for a Loach, ID number Bravo 519." He settled in his seat as if he were going on a Sunday drive. "You have your destination. Make this easy."

A helicopter takeoff under fire from a squad of MP's, was frightening; attempting to put a man on the deck of a pitching freighter far out to sea had been nerve-racking; but for sheer heart-in-the-mouth terror, Walter Salt found that both paled when compared with landing a helicopter on a suburban street.

As the chopper came down, Salt couldn't see any room for his aircraft: the houses seemed to be packed together on their small quarter-acre lots, cars—station wagons and minivans mostly—were parked on the streets, lawns were scattered with bicycles and other kids' toys, and the whole area seemed to be knit together in a web of telephone and electrical lines. There wasn't a lot of room for error.

Salt positioned the aircraft directly over the strip of asphalt and then lowered the cyclic and cut back on the throttles. The chopper dropped like a stone, hit and bounced, then hit and bounced again.

Salt opened his eyes. "Man . . ." He sighed. "This is gonna take years off my life."

Sam Daniels didn't care. While Salt was shutting down the engines he grabbed the duffel bag and jumped out of the cabin, running for the Jeffries house.

Kate and her mother were standing on the front porch, both of them staring wide-eyed at the helicopter and the men who had dropped from the sky, shattering the calm of their peaceful neighborhood.

"Mrs. Jeffries? I'm Colonel Daniels. This is Major Salt," said Sam quickly. "We sure are grateful you called, ma'am. Have you seen the animal today?"

"No," said Mrs. Jeffries. "Kate usually puts out some scraps for it. But today—" The woman shrugged her shoulders apologetically.

"Where does it usually come out?"

"In the backyard."

"Okay," said Sam, trying to keep his voice calm. "Do you think you could put together a plate of whatever it is you usually put out . . ."

"Of course." Mrs. Jeffries pulled her daughter back into the house as Salt and Daniels raced around to the rear.

They surveyed the swatch of lawn, like field marshals examining a battleground. There was nothing out of the ordinary there—a swing set, a redwood picnic table, a stump where a tree had been cut down—and there was no sign of the monkey either. Salt opened a case and started assembling a single-shot tranquilizer gun, feeding the lethal-looking dart into the chamber. He cocked and pumped the gun ready to take down the animal.

Mrs. Jeffries scurried out of the house, holding a plate piled high with fruit and cookies. "This is usually what Katie gives her. I hope it's all right . . ."

"I'm sure it's fine, Mrs. Jeffries," said Sam. "If I could ask you to wait in the house. Major Salt will stay with you."

"Okay," said Mrs. Jeffries, tossing an uncertain sidelong glance at Salt.

As she started back toward the house, Sam pulled Salt aside and whispered instructions quickly. "I'm gonna put the goodies on that stump. Can you get a shot from the kitchen window?"

Salt drew a mental line from the window to the tree stump. "Yeah. Should be easy."

"Good. Get in there . . . And Salt, don't let anyone in or out."

"Right."

The next thirty minutes passed in silence and frustration. Sam Daniels hid himself behind a tree, his eyes fixed on the plate of scraps twenty yards away. The stillness was profound, the hush so overwhelming it could almost be heard—and Sam wanted to scream in frustration.

Salt rested the barrel of his weapon on the windowsill in the kitchen, his sights fixed on the tree stump. Mrs. Jeffries waited with him, staring in the same direction.

"She won't come," said Kate in a small voice.

Salt looked down at her. "Are you sure? Why won't she come, Kate?"

"She won't come," said Kate firmly. "Except to me . . ."

**Beale Air Force Base
Marysville, California**

SEPTEMBER 6, 1995, 4:12 P.M.

Two F-15 fighter bombers stood on the runway at Beale AFB awaiting the order for takeoff. Harnessed under each wing were canisters of high pressure incendiary explosives, the fuel air bomb—enough combustible material to incinerate Cedar Creek three times over.

The run would be a simple one. The two aircraft would approach the town from the east. At a predetermined point six miles from the outer perimeter, the jets were to cut southeast and approach the town from due south, dropping to a bombing altitude of seven thousand feet. At that point the canisters were to be dropped, pressure-set to explode just one hundred feet above the ground. The canisters would break open, expelling hundreds and hundreds of bomblets which would detonate, further discharging more explosive.

In a matter of seconds the entire area of Cedar Creek would be covered with a field of deadly material which would erupt into a huge cloud of fire. Anything it touched would burn—and it would touch everything.

The pilots knew exactly what they were doing and they weren't happy about it. The argument that "Orders were orders" did not seem to wash here; they were unleashing a terrible power on their own people and the pilots were uneasy in their cockpits.

Without warning, General Ford's voice crackled in their headphones. "Gentlemen . . ." he said, "the President has issued his final authorization for this operation. We are ordered to proceed."

The pilot of the lead F-15, designated Sandman One, grimaced when he heard the news. He could imagine how this was playing to his weapon systems operator, seated directly behind him in the cockpit, or to the two guys in the other plane. The pilot knew that nothing could backfire quite as spectacularly as a pep talk from the higher ups.

"Shit," he whispered. He had been hoping up to the last minute that the operation would not come to pass after all.

"I know that each of us has his doubts about what we have been ordered to do," Ford continued. "We'd be less than human if we didn't have these doubts. We've been commanded to take the lives of human beings."

Sandman Two, the wing man on the operation, swore as well. "Had to go and remind us . . ."

Ford felt he had to put some steel into the pilots, to try to make them understand that they were undertaking a mission that *had* to be performed. "The fate of the nation and perhaps the whole world is in our hands. We are the last line of defense. We did not seek such a terrible burden . . ."

"Hell no," said Sandman One.

"But we cannot refuse it," said Ford, speaking with a conviction he was not sure he could sustain. "I have faith that each of us . . . each of you . . . will do his duty. God bless us all." Ford switched off his mike and sat alone in his darkened office. "And may God forgive us . . ."

17

SEPTEMBER 6, 1995, 4:15 P.M.

Sam Daniels knelt down next to Kate Jeffries and looked into the little girl's eyes. He could see that she was very scared and confused, completely perplexed by the mysterious goings-on around her. For his own part, Sam was nervous and anxious—the whole operation had come down to this, life and death hinging on the cooperation of this little girl and her ability to cajole a frightened beast out of its lair.

"Katie," he asked slowly, "have you ever been sick?"

Kate Jeffries nodded gravely. "Uh-huh."

"Then I guess you know it's not much fun, is it?"

She shook her head again. "Uh-uh."

"Well," he said, "a whole lot of people are very sick right now. My wife is sick. My friend . . . And Betsy can help make them better, because she's very special—you know she's special, don't you?"

Kate nodded again, her fingers twirling in her hair. "She's special," she agreed.

In the background, Salt glanced at his watch. Precious minutes were ticking away.

Sam took a deep breath. "So, we've got to take her with us in our helicopter, and we need your help to get Betsy to come along with us. Understand?"

"Are you going to hurt her?" Kate asked solemnly. "You wouldn't hurt her, would you?"

Sam shook his head vigorously. "No, no . . . we're just going to make her go to sleep, that's all."

"Go to sleep? Why?"

"So Betsy won't be scared in the helicopter," said Sam quickly.

Kate considered this for a moment. "You promise you won't hurt her?"

"I promise," said Sam, crossing his heart. "If she gets hurt you can punch me in the nose."

Kate looked at Sam for a long time, then looked over to her mother. Then she nodded. "Okay," she said.

"Good," said Sam. "Come on . . ."

Salt knelt behind some shrubbery in the backyard, watching as the little girl walked across the lawn, half an apple clutched in her hand. Only now did he ready his rifle—he had kept it hidden until now, for fear of frightening Katie.

At the edge of the woods she stopped and peered into the underbrush. "Betsy," Katie called. "Betsy . . ."

At first, there was no response—only a maddening stillness. In the house, Mrs. Jeffries and Sam watched, the suspense intense and agonizing.

Kate called again. "Betsy . . . C'mon, Betsy."

This time a rustling sound could be heard and a shadowy figure came creeping forward, not from the woods directly in front of her, but a few yards to the left. The monkey paused in the undergrowth, scanning the backyard.

Salt brought his rifle up, putting his eye to the scope. He could see the monkey—but the little girl was directly in the line of fire. He crept a few feet to his left, praying that his movement would not spook the animal. He leaned up against a section of fence and raised his rifle again.

Kate waved the apple at the monkey. "Come on, girl," said Kate. "It's okay." Kate walked a few feet closer—closer than planned. Salt pushed himself against the fence, trying to get a clean line to the animal.

Kate's arm was extended as far as it could go and Betsy was reaching for the apple— when the fence post gave way with a sharp crack.

Betsy jumped and turned, hissing furiously. Kate's hand was frozen in fear, the monkey's teeth only inches from the little girl's flesh.

"Fire goddammit," whispered Sam. "Shoot already."

Salt had stopped breathing. He sighted his target in the scope, catching a flash of black fur just long enough to squeeze off a shot. He fired. The tranquilizer dart sliced through the air, just missing Kate and striking Betsy in the leg. The monkey jumped straight into the air, screaming in pain, shock, and fear. But the narcotic was a powerful one and the animal was knocked out before it hit the ground.

"Betsy!" Instinctively, the little girl moved to comfort the animal.

"No!" yelled Sam racing across the lawn. He grabbed Kate and swept her away from the monkey. "No, Katie, you can't touch her."

"You hurt her!" Kate wailed. "You said you wouldn't hurt her and you did!"

Sam put her down gently. "We didn't hurt her, honey," he said. "She's just sleeping, that's all."

The sound of approaching choppers began to fill the air. Salt turned and looked into the sky. "Uh, sir?"

"I know," he said over his shoulder. "We got company. Get the monkey to the chopper—and put on your seat belt." He turned back to Katie. "Betsy's okay, I promise. We had to do it that way to make her go to sleep. She'll be all right because I'm gonna make sure that—"

That's as far as he got. Kate had summoned up all the strength she could and punched Sam right in the nose.

"Ow!" The little girl had taken him completely by surprise. Sam rubbed his nose. "Okay," he said with a smile. "I guess I deserved that."

Mrs. Jeffries enfolded her daughter in a hug, holding her tight so she wouldn't see Salt slip on a pair of gloves and put the monkey in the duffel.

"She's upset," said Sam apologetically. "I'm terribly sorry. Can you handle her?" He glanced over at Salt, who was climbing into the chopper. A moment later the rotors began to turn. "I'm sorry . . . I have to go."

McClintock's Huey helicopter roared over the scene, the second chopper right behind him. He looked down, saw the Loach—as incongruous as a UFO on that suburban street—and turned to his pilot.

"Unless Honda dealers are now selling OH-6 Loach helicopters, that would be our man." The two Hueys went into a tight bank left and came back toward the Loach.

"Tighten your sphincter, mister," McClintock said with a cackle. "We are in pursuit."

Salt didn't think twice about the takeoff. It wasn't that the maneuver was any less difficult—this time he was too scared to worry and too determined to let this thing end now. They had the monkey. It was time to bring it back to Cedar Creek.

The Loach was moving north over the treetops on a dead run for the town. Sam was on his cellular phone, shouting over the screaming engines.

"Briggs!" he yelled. "Put General Ford on the phone, now. Tell him it's Colonel Daniels."

Billy Ford picked up immediately. "Sam! Where the hell are you?"

"I'm in the air." He peered down at a ribbon of highway. "I'm not sure where exactly. We've got the host, Billy. We found it."

"Thank God," said Ford. Sam could hear the general's sigh of relief over the phone. "Are you sure it's the right one?"

Sam nodded. "Yes, she's it. You've got to call off the bombing."

"I'll try to buy you some time," Ford replied. "That's all I can do. You just get your ass back here quickly, safely. Got it, Sam?"

"Yes, sir."

"Ah, Sam?"

"Yes, General?"

"You might encounter some resistance on your journey back," he said. "Be aware of that."

In the big outrigger mirrors on the side of the Loach he could see small black dots behind them. They were getting bigger and assuming the shape of heavily armed helicopters. "Thanks for the warning."

He broke the connection and turned to Salt. "We've got company," said Sam.

"You said that already," Salt replied.

Sam craned his head to get a look at the pursuit craft. "Have you read this chapter, Salt?"

Salt shook his head slowly. "Sorry to tell you this, sir, but this chapter wasn't in the book."

"I asked you to work on that reassurance thing, Salt."

"Just as soon as I have a minute, sir."

Salt kicked up the throttles and pushed the chopper down, following the course of a narrow riverbed. As if in a game of follow the leader the two Hueys lost altitude and dropped too, but then they gained height and lifted up over and away from the river, vanishing into the blue sky.

Sam looked back. The twin pursuit choppers were nowhere to be seen. "I think we lost them," he said, bewildered. "That was too easy . . ."

He was right. Like attack dogs, the choppers were on the scent of the Loach again.

"They're back," said Salt. "Dammit." The two helicopters gained on the Loach, flying in escort formation.

"Army 1-3-5-0, Viper lead." The pilot's voice filled their ears. "We are at your six o'clock. Acknowledge."

Salt nodded. "Viper lead, this is Army. I hear you."

McClintock took over the radio. "Army 1-3-5-0, you will allow us to escort you to Travis Air Force Base, where you will be placed in quarantine."

Sam seized the microphone. "We are headed back to Cedar Creek with the host animal and do not require escort."

"We will escort you, Colonel Daniels," said McClintock. "Do not make it difficult."

"Who has given this directive?"

"I have, Daniels. General McClintock. Acknowledge."

"What the hell? Salt, we've got a two-star general on our ass—"

"Great."

"General," Sam radioed, "I've got the host. We can make the serum, we can save these people."

McClintock was unmoved. "Colonel Daniels, you will follow us to Travis for quarantine. We will take care of the animal. Acknowledge."

Sam was incredulous. "God, he's still talking quarantine when *we've* got the host." He picked up the mike again. "General, I will not allow this animal out of my sight until I am back in Cedar Creek. Acknowledge *that*."

"If you do not come willingly," said McClintock, "we will force you to go to Travis."

Sam lost his temper. "General, I beg your pardon, but who the hell is sick at Travis Air Force Base? Why are you depriving twenty-six hundred people of the only known source of the antiserum?"

"Daniels," said McClintock ominously, "you leave me no choice."

The Hueys broke off and dropped behind and above the Loach. "Colonel, they're setting up for the kill," said Salt.

"You can go to hell, General!" Sam shouted into the microphone. Then he shut down the radio. "Salt, get us the hell out of here . . ."

"Okay. Banking left and down. Hold on, sir." The chopper lost altitude rapidly, diving down so low the skids seemed to skim the riverbed.

"What are you doing?" asked Sam, alarmed.

"Don't want to give 'em a clear shot, sir."

"What do you mean, clear shot?"

"They got weapons, sir."

Two bridges spanned the river ahead of them. One was the more modern road bridge, beyond was the older railway trestle. The viaduct was festooned with electrical wires, lowering the clearance by a full ten feet.

All three chopper pilots looked at the obstacle and assessed their positions. The commander of Huey Two was the most realistic of the trio.

"I can't clear those wires—I'm breaking off. I'm breaking off." The chopper peeled away to the left, dropping out of the chase.

McClintock watched his backup break off and turned to his own pilot. "Stay with him, mister," he ordered. "And don't ask me to hold your hand."

Salt didn't know what to do. He could not take his eyes off the bridges—but he couldn't make up his mind.

"Over or under, sir? Over or under?"

Sam was gripping the sides of his seat, his knuckles turning white. "How the hell should I know," he said, terrified. "I'm a virologist."

Salt decided at the last minute. The Loach zoomed under the bridge, the rotors almost brushing the stone stanchions. Before they could recover from the shock of having made it through, they flashed beneath the arches of the second bridge.

The Huey was still right behind them, firing continuously now. Salt threw the Loach left, then right, his best attempt at evasive flying. But he knew it was only a matter of time before the pilot drew a bead on him and blasted him out of the sky.

Sam was still frozen in his seat, the landscape whirling around him until he wasn't sure which way was up and which was down.

"This is *not* why I joined the Army," he screamed into the wind.

"Me neither!" He gripped the yoke a little tighter. It was time for some daring. At full power, he pushed the helicopter straight into the air, a total vertical climb, the Huey One roaring away beneath it. At the top of the climb, Salt whipped the Loach around in a full 180-degree turn, dropped a hundred feet and raced back the way he had come.

"Jesus, Salt! Warn me before you pull a stunt like that, will ya?"

Salt was dumbfounded at what had happened. "I didn't know I was gonna do it until it was done, sir . . ."

McClintock was not a happy camper. "Viper Two, where the hell are you?"

"Viper Two rejoining, sir, catching up."

"Well, you should know that target has reversed direction," McClintock advised. "He's coming back at you."

The pilot looked straight ahead. The Loach was in his path, coming straight at him. "I've got him," he reported. "He's coming directly at me."

It had developed into an aerial game of chicken. The choppers were on dead collision courses. All that remained to be seen was whose nerve would shatter first.

The Huey pilot's hands were locked on his joystick and he could barely stand to watch. "Holy shit!"

But, suddenly, it seemed that it was Salt

who didn't have the guts to finish the game he had started. He pulled up, yanking the chopper into the air. Once he was gone the two Hueys realized they had been outsmarted. With the Loach gone the two attack helicopters were flying directly toward each other, on a collision course, only seconds away from impact.

Both aircraft banked right, swinging way off course, but only missing each other by a few feet. They clattered off over the tree line, both pilots fighting for control.

Sam wiped the sweat from his face and watched as the confused pursuers were forced to break off the hunt.

"This thing have rockets?"

"I'm not shooting them down," said Salt. "I don't know *how* to shoot them down."

"I don't want you to. Just shoot a couple of rockets into the trees."

Salt caught the strategy immediately. "Right." He flipped open the firing box and pressed the button hard. The Loach rocked as the two missiles blasted off and raced ahead, erupting in the forest. They couldn't hear the detonations, but they could see the effects, a ball of flame and smoke billowing into the air.

"Where the hell'd he go?" McClintock demanded.

His pilot picked up the pillar of smoke. "Look there, sir . . ."

McClintock saw the smoke and smiled. "Looks like the son of a bitch has run out of luck. Let's go down and take a look . . ."

"I think they bought it, sir," said Salt. They were both shaken and out of breath. "Good call, sir."

"Let's get this monkey to the hospital," Sam yelled. He reached back and tapped the duffel. "How you doing back there, Betsy? Your visit to the States been pleasant so far?"

18

The parking lot of the hospital was deserted, so that's where they landed. They were back in Cedar Creek, less than twelve hours after it had taken off, yet Salt found it hard to believe it was actually the same day. The engine was running rough, the tail was riddled with bullet holes and there was nothing left in the fuel tank but fumes, but they had made it. Now they could go back to being doctors.

The base was completely deserted, all traces of the military presence had disappeared except for the command center and a few vehicles abandoned on the streets. The only sound came from the loudspeakers, continuing to broadcast those bland messages of assurance.

"The rats have definitely left the ship," said Salt, climbing out of the Loach.

"Yeah," said Sam. "And now they're going to sink it." He hefted the duffel bag and tapped it. "Up to you now, you little shit . . ."

A few minutes later the two men were back in their Racal biosafety suits, Salt in the BL-4 lab doing what he did best—working with blood and tissue, culturing the material from Betsy's veins into a lifesaving compound.

Working carefully but quickly, Salt attached tubes from a blood separator into the intravenous ports that he had already inserted into the unconscious body of Betsy. Blood pumped along the plastic tubing and into the machine, where the liquid then passed into the centrifuges. There it was spun thousands of times a second, separating the antibodies that Salt would work into anti-serum.

While Salt worked, Sam went in search of Robby. The hospital was still crammed with the sick and dying and a few nurses did their best to tend to them. Ruiz and Aronson moved from bed to bed, but they were so exhausted they moved with the jerky motions of automatons.

He found Casey first. He was riddled with Motaba, only just barely conscious and gasping for breath. His eyes were open but he did not seem to recognize his friend. Sam took his hand.

"Case," he said. "It's me. It's Sam."

Casey blinked, as if attempting to focus his eyes and his thoughts. "Sam? Who's Sam?"

"Sam, the dumb guy. Your friend . . ."

A light came into Casey's dull eyes as he realized who was speaking to him. For a moment, his features softened and he found the strength to push away his pain. He reached up and touched his fingertips to the visor of Sam's helmet.

"Take it easy, Case," Sam whispered. "Save

your strength, you'll be okay . . ." He knew
he was lying. Even if the serum had been
ready right at that moment, Sam could see
that Casey was too far gone, the organ damage too great.

"Sam . . . Sam . . ." he gasped. "I *hate* this
bug. I hate it."

Casey lay back and closed his eyes, his life
slipping away as Sam watched. Schuler's last
words had been an exhortation. He was urg-
ing his friend to cure Motaba, to take his
revenge on the disease that had taken his life.

Robby lay in bed in another ward. Her face
was flushed with fever, her eyes red, her skin
covered with the Motaba lesions. She was
conscious enough to recognize Sam and she
smiled as he sat by her bed and took her bare
hand in his gloved one.

"You're back," she said.

"I said I would be."

"How's Casey?" Robby asked.

"He's gonna be okay," Sam said quickly.
"You're both gonna be okay. We found the
host."

"You don't have to lie to me, Sam," she said. "Casey is dead, isn't he?"

Tears came into Sam's eyes. He couldn't lie, but his silence told her that she was right. "Poor Casey," she whispered.

"*You* are going to live," Sam said. "We found the host, Robby, we'll have the antiserum, so you can't give up."

Suddenly, she was afraid. "Just hold me . . . I need you near me, Sam."

Sam tried to enfold her in his arms, but the embrace was clumsy and awkward in his biosafety suit. "You're going to make it, Rob. Okay? Promise me . . ." But it was as if she had only needed to see him again, to say goodbye. She closed her eyes and sighed.

"Dammit, Robby, don't! Don't leave," he said frantically. "I've got to . . . Robby, dammit!"

His voice was muffled through the visor and she seemed to be drifting away. He started to strip off his suit, tearing off his helmet and throwing it to the floor, the gloves followed and he pulled her close to him, as if trying to transfer his strength and health to her.

"Robby . . . Robby . . . C'mon."

His voice roused her and she opened her eyes, looking surprised to see him exposed. "Sam . . ." she gasped. "What are you doing?"

"We're going to make it. The antiserum is going to work. I need you, Robby."

"That's a stupid way to make your point," she said, a flash of the old Robby showing through. "It had better work, huh? Who's gonna take care of Helen and Louis?"

Sam leaned down and kissed her hot skin. "We both will. Right? We both will."

A smile on her face, Robby began to drift off again, sinking further into the black hole of her illness.

"Robby . . . don't go . . . answer me—we both will, right?" Sam grabbed her by the shoulders as if trying to shake her back to consciousness. "Dammit, don't die on me now . . . don't do this, please . . ."

Salt sprinted into the room, holding a plastic bag. "Sir—" His mouth dropped open when he realized that Sam had stripped off his suit. "You got a lot of faith in this stuff, sir."

"Set it up, Salt."

Together they hooked the serum bag up to the IV drip and then watched as the milky liquid flowed down the tube and into Robby's arm.

Then Sam sat down on the bed and held Robby's hand, watching and waiting. Salt stood at a distance and found it difficult to hold back his tears. . . .

The hours passed, the deadline for the bombing came and went—Billy Ford was making good on his promise to buy some time—but the serum appeared to have had no effect. Robby remained comatose and hope was dripping away like the liquid in the IV tube.

The elation at finding the host, at being given a chance to win, had drained out of Sam. He was enough of a realist to know that there was nothing more he could do. Eventually, McClintock would prevail and the bomb run would be launched.

With a sigh, he stood up and pulled a piece of paper from his Racal suit and handed it to Salt. "Take this," he said.

"What is it?"

"A signed declaration that you were following my orders at all times." He thrust the paper into Salt's hand. "Now take it and get out of here."

Salt shook his head. "No."

"Do it, Salt. Just do it. There's got to be someone left who knows the truth. You'll be the only one left."

"But, sir—"

"Go, Major. That's an order."

Salt looked at Sam for a long moment, too moved to speak. Gently, Sam turned him around and pushed him toward the exit.

"We're fine here," he said. "Go."

Mobile Command Center

9:21 RM.

McClintock stood over Billy Ford, staring down angrily at him. He shook his head. "Why, Billy?"

"Because I believe we can still save these people," he said. "That's why."

"You *believe*?" McClintock almost laughed. "You believe that because Daniels flies in here with a monkey tucked under his arm that you can put this genie back in the bottle? What's the matter with you, Billy?"

"Talk about genies in bottles!" said Ford angrily. "Motaba is useless as a weapon now, Donny, even you must see that."

McClintock took an aluminum case from the pocket of his fatigues and laid it on the desk. "I know much better than that, General. I don't want to see these people die. But they're dead already. We both know that. I gave you a direct order, authorized by the White House."

Ford did not look impressed. "The White House? How much did you reveal?"

"No more than they wanted to know," said McClintock dismissively.

"We had the antiserum and we didn't use it. You don't think this is going to come out?"

"Who's going to tell, Billy?" McClintock asked. "You?"

"Daniels," said Ford. "Daniels knows all

about it. He knows about the people we killed in Africa."

McClintock smirked. "And where is Daniels now." He pointed out the window. "Down there, right? Doing his job. You should have been doing yours. You lost your nerve. I'm disappointed in you, Billy. Thought you had more backbone than that." McClintock shook his head and then walked toward the radio console in the corner of the office.

Ford jumped to his feet and blocked his path. "Give him more time."

"Move, General," said McClintock firmly. "That's an order."

"Give him more time, or—"

McClintock pulled a sidearm from the holster on his belt. "Or what, Billy? Time is up. Have a seat."

But Ford held his ground. McClintock moved forward and put the muzzle of the gun to Ford's forehead. Then, very coolly, he picked up the radio microphone and clicked it into life.

"Sandman One, this is Viper One . . ."

All afternoon and into the evening the two F-15's had been sitting on the runway at

Beale Air Force Base waiting for the order to stand down or proceed. Both the pilot and the WSO were so bored they were almost asleep and it took a moment for the pilot to respond.

"Sandman One to Viper One, standing by, over."

"You are to proceed with Operation Clean Sweep immediately," said McClintock crisply. "You will make two runs. Over."

"That's a roger, Viper One. Sandman out."

"Viper out . . ." McClintock turned back to Ford. "Now, it'll be just you and me again, Billy. Just you and me."

Ford shook his head. "I don't think so, Donny. Not this time."

McClintock laughed. "Okay, General. Follow your conscience. Take the fall. Take me down with you. That's part of the game, isn't it?" He laughed a little more. "Aw, hell, four years down the line you'll be running for Senator. I'll even vote for you. Now sit down, would ya'? My arm is getting tired . . ."

The bag of antiserum was empty. Sam looked at it for a moment, then looked down at

Robby. She had not stirred for hours, though she continued to breathe.

Slowly, gradually, Sam became aware of a sound, the vibrating whine of jet engines. He knew what was coming.

Sam reached for Robby's hand and held it tightly, resigning himself to her fate and his. He closed his eyes and waited. . . .

But then he felt something . . . Robby was weakly squeezing his hand. Sam opened his eyes and saw that she was staring up at him.

"Sam?"

"Robby!"

The sound of the planes was louder now, growing in intensity. The air started to quiver. "Robby," he said quickly. "Don't talk. Stay awake. Okay? Stay awake now . . ." He kissed her hand and started to run.

Cedar Creek, California

Zero Hour

Sam slapped his pockets looking for his cellular phone, but he had misplaced it somewhere. The phones in the nurses' station were dead, so he rushed outside to the chopper, praying he could contact the planes. The sound of the engines was much louder now, closing fast on the town.

He threw open the door of the Loach and grabbed the radio mike, fumbling with the buttons, turning it on and switching to the secure air traffic channel. The F-15's were dots on the horizon, but growing larger by the second.

"Stop!" Sam screamed. "Stop the attack! We've found the antiserum and it works! Do you read?"

There was no response. The silence from the advancing aircraft was terrifying, dreadful.

"Do you hear me?" Daniels shouted frantically. "This is Colonel Daniels . . . we have the means to save these people. Do you read?"

For a very long moment there was nothing

but static on the radio, then the pilot of the lead jet broke the radio silence. "We read, sir."

Sam's heart leaped and then fell—McClintock's voice broke into the radio traffic, sounding like the voice of God. "This is General McClintock," he said sternly. "I order you to ignore this man. You will proceed with the mission!"

Sam did the acting job of his life. "General! Thank God you're there. I've been trying to reach you. We have new data. I know you'll be relieved to learn that we don't have to bomb the town."

McClintock did not sound relieved. "Sandman One, ignore this man. He is a criminal. Proceed with the mission as ordered!"

The F-15's had made their turn to the south and were dead-on for the town, closing fast. "Sandman! We can save these people! This is a fact. The general is only now learning that the antiserum has been found."

"I have all the data," said McClintock. "Proceed, Sandman. If you do not you will be shot for dereliction of duty—"

"Bullshit! You can't do that, General. Please, Sandman, listen to me."

Suddenly another voice cut into the traffic. It was Billy Ford. He had torn the microphone from McClintock's hands and was speaking fast.

"Colonel Daniels is right, Sandman. This is General Ford. I have seen the data and I have orders from the President that—"

McClintock was in no mood to fool around. He cold-cocked Ford with the handle of his sidearm, knocking him out. He snatched back the microphone. "Sandman One, both of these men are lying. General Ford has been placed under arrest. You are to proceed with the mission as directed."

The pilots of the two jets were as confused as they had ever been. Sam looked up at the planes, as if talking directly to them.

"We can save these people." His voice was hoarse with desperation. "I promise you that. Do not drop your bombs. If you do, you'll have to live with your decision for the rest of your lives. And it is now your decision . . ."

"It is not your decision!" McClintock

roared. "You have your orders and you will follow them!"

"The orders have been revoked! Do not kill these people—" Daniels' voice cut out abruptly as McClintock shut down his transmission. He could hear but he could no longer broadcast.

"This is General McClintock . . ." He sounded as if he had regained his composure. "I am in charge here. Proceed with the mission. Do you read me, Sandman?"

There was a long silence, then Sandman One came back on the air. "We read you, General. We are approaching the target . . .

The jets had their noses down and they were screaming toward the bomb point. "Oh Jesus . . ." Sam whispered. "Oh my God . . ."

The air was filled with the sound of the howling engines. Daniels could see the canisters under the wings quite clearly and he hunched his shoulders and winced, expecting to see them drop. But the jets passed over the town low and tight, wing tip to wing tip, as if flying over in salute.

"Sandman! What is happening! You are disobeying a direct order."

"Sir," said the pilot, "there seems to be some sort of malfunction, something is wrong with my release mechanism . . ."

Sandman Two came on the air. "Helluva thing, sir, I seem to have the same damn problem . . ."

EPILOGUE

The lesions were fading from Robby's skin and her face regained a pink and healthy pallor. When she opened her eyes she still felt weak and infirm, but she could tell she was on the mend.

Sam, on the other hand, looked terrible. His face was drawn, drained of color, and there were deep, dark circles under his eyes.

"Jeez, Sam," said Robby with a small smile, "you really look like shit."

"Yeah, rough day at work . . . How are you doing?"

"I don't know, Doc. You tell me. Give it to me straight."

Sam smiled gently. "You beat it," he said. "Or rather we beat it."

"We did?"

Sam nodded. "Yes we did. We're evacuating now; every patient has the antiserum. Some of them won't make it . . . but a lot of them will."

The image of Sam without his Racal biosafety suit came back to her. "Hope you got your shots, Sam."

"Yeah. I did. And you know how I hate shots. I don't trust doctors, either. Had to do it myself."

"I don't understand, how did you generate the antiserum so quickly?"

"Betsy saved you."

"Betsy?"

"The monkey, the host, bless her heart. Salt was able to reproduce the antiserum by synthesizing her antibodies with the plasma from M-2 patients and E-1101—"

Robby waved him off. "Shop talk. Save it. Let's call this our day off."

"We got lucky, Rob," said Sam soberly. "That made all the difference."

"Well, you gotta count on luck sometimes."

"Yeah, you do, don't you . . . You had me scared."

"Good," she said with a smile.

He leaned closer to her. "What was it like? I mean, here we are, fighting it from the outside, right? Watching it. And then, you're fighting it from the inside."

"This is morbid, Sam . . . And it's more shop talk."

"Tell me," Sam insisted.

"You're not my boss anymore, Sam."

"I never was, Rob. Tell me . . ."

Robby thought for a moment. "I was dizzy first. Then I got scared. Really scared. Something was moving through me—this thing I was trying to figure out. I thought I was going to die if I didn't get rid of it. Then I accepted it. I knew what it was and I accepted it. But I wasn't going to give in . . ." She smiled and winked at him. "It was sort of like living with you."

Sam laughed. "Thanks a lot."

"You asked," she said simply. "It was a unique experience."

"Would you do it again?"

"Do what?"

They both knew that they weren't talking about the illness now.

"I think I might," said Robby. "Now that I have the antibodies."

Sam took Robby's hand in his and squeezed. "It's your day off, Robby. Not mine. I should get back to work. They need help out there."

Robby nodded. "Go."

Cedar Creek had not been bombed, but it had ceased to exist nonetheless. The decision had been made to evacuate the town completely, every man, woman, and child, infected or not, was being taken away from the town for resettlement elsewhere. Sherry Mauldin, weak and wasted, responded slowly to the treatment, but she knew she would recover—she knew the instant she was reunited with her family.

Buses and military transport trucks left the staging areas, every few seconds filled with walking wounded, each of them clutching an antiserum IV.

The tent city was being broken up. Most of the beds were empty and the tents have been struck, sitting in the field like wilted flowers.

Once the town was evacuated, Sandman One and Sandman Two were scrambled and this time they went through with the bomb run, making two devastating passes over Cedar Creek, reducing the hamlet to a vast inferno.

From far beyond the outer perimeter Sam Daniels watched the angry flames climb into the sky and was reminded of the old military aphorism: sometimes it was necessary to destroy a town in order to save it.

The Center for Disease Control announced the following day that the Motaba virus had been contained in Cedar Creek and that work had begun on the production of synthetic antibodies.

Not long after that McClintock, Ford, and Daniels testified at Senate hearings on the outbreak of the disease. Although severely reprimanded, McClintock and Ford were permitted to retain their posts. Sam Daniels resigned his commission.

Just over a month later the CDC issued a press release announcing that Dr. Sam Daniels had taken a job as senior virologist at the Center for Disease Control, where he was going to work under the direct supervision of . . . Dr. Roberta Keough. The press release did not mention that Sam and Robby had been remarried the week before.

All the clutter from Sam's bachelor apartment was boxed up and sent south to their new home, along with his few pieces of furniture. All of his belongings were harmoniously incorporated into the new setting: Robby's and Sam's books were reunited and the photographs went back on the shelves and the bedside table.

Not so lucky, however, was Sam's couch. It was stained, Robby pointed out, and it smelled of wet dog. On the first day off from the CDC, the newlyweds shopped for a new couch.

They agreed on style, fabric, and design,

but they could find no common ground on where it should be positioned in their living room.

Sam wanted it under the window. Robby didn't. "No, Sam. The light's going to hit it all day. The fabric'll fade . . . Let's have it next to the fireplace."

"Shit, Robby, it's only a couch."

"An expensive couch," Robby retorted. "You want it to last, don't you?"

The dogs didn't care where the couch sat. Without warning, they jumped up onto the cushions and made themselves comfortable. Robby looked, sighed, and shook her head.

"Louis," she said firmly. "Down."

Instantly, the dogs climbed down. Robby flashed a triumphant smile at her husband. "See?"

"That's because you had 'em for so long," said Sam. "You brainwashed them."

"So it begins . . ." groaned Robby. She put her shoulder to the couch and started moving it toward the fireplace. Sam watched her a moment. "Here," he said. "Let me give you a hand . . ."